"Who are you and why are you helping me?"

"Lieutenant Micah Kent, head of the naval dolphin training program here in Coronado." He extended a hand.

"Pleased to meet you," Keilani said.

He nodded, thinking to return the sentiment, but the unexpected ping of a gunshot sent him into action instead.

Keilani cried out. He pushed her just out of the line of fire as he urged her to run. A trickle of blood ran down her arm. She slapped a hand over the top of it but kept moving. She didn't even look at the wound.

"Head for that green door on your right." He pulled his government-issue SIG from his belt, turned and fired in the direction from which the shots had come.

To his surprise, he heard shots right behind him, and turned to find Keilani firing her own weapon with precision and confidence. He blinked as he opened the door. He'd had no idea she had a weapon hidden away in that wet suit.

Jerking her inside, he slammed the door behind them. "Nice." He nodded at her.

"What? You expected a panicked damsel?"

Sommer Smith teaches high school English and loves animals. She loves reading romances and writing about fairy tales. She started writing her first novel when she was thirteen and has wanted to write romances since. Her three children provide her inspiration to write with their many antics. With two dogs and a horse to keep her active in between, Sommer stays busy traveling to ball games and colleges in two states.

Books by Sommer Smith

Love Inspired Suspense

Under Suspicion

UNDER SUSPICION

SOMMER SMITH

LOVE INSPIRED SUSPENSE
INSPIRATIONAL ROMANCE

LOVE INSPIRED®SUSPENSE
INSPIRATIONAL ROMANCE

ISBN-13: 978-1-335-40301-8

Recycling programs
for this product may
not exist in your area.

Under Suspicion

This edition published by arrangement with Harlequin Books S.A.

For questions and comments about the quality of this book, please contact us at CustomerService@Harlequin.com.

Love Inspired
22 Adelaide St. West, 40th Floor
Toronto, Ontario M5H 4E3, Canada
www.Harlequin.com

Printed in U.S.A.

Now unto him that is able to do exceeding abundantly above all that we ask or think, according to the power that worketh in us, unto him be glory in the church by Christ Jesus throughout all ages, world without end. Amen.

–*Ephesians* 3:20-21

This book is dedicated to the memory
of my late grandmother, Estle Chisum, who always
quietly and steadfastly believed in my dreams.
She earnestly believed that we are all
exactly who we make up our minds to be.

ONE

Locked.

Keilani knew she should have expected as much. This navy SEAL base had top-notch military security, after all. It didn't matter that she was something of an expert at getting through barriers. She wouldn't take the risk of going inside without permission. She wasn't here to cause trouble, only to get a sense of the layout before her job working with the dolphins started.

All she wanted was a little sneak preview of what she would be working with—any prior knowledge she could arm herself with would help. New situations had always been difficult for her, and she merely wanted to familiarize herself with the area, perhaps relieve her anxiety just a little bit. The admiral had assured her it was safe for her to look around.

She uttered a little prayer for strength. Men in uniform still made her nervous, after all that had happened, but the job had been too good to turn down. She had overcome this type of situation before and she could do it again.

And the dolphins needed her, especially if she found out the rumors were true. She owed it to her friend

Gretchen at the World Animal Protection Agency to investigate. If not for Gretchen, she might not have made it through vet school.

Keilani had held a deep affection for dolphins since she was a tiny girl. She hoped to discover it was all just a big misunderstanding, but she was determined to know for sure.

With no other option left to her, Keilani decided to take a swim. From the layout of the base's SEAL training facilities, there were only two likely locations where the dolphins might be housed. The fences of the navy base extended far out and around the actual buildings, so the only way she might get a look without an escort would be by way of the water. There was no close beach access, though, so getting there from outside wouldn't be an easy feat. Fortunately, she was a very strong swimmer.

The sand was warm and a bit rough beneath her bare feet. The water was clear and cool today and no one seemed to be about. Did the navy patrol this particular section of the beach? She couldn't be sure, so if she didn't want to be questioned about her reasons for being there by more uniforms, she would be wise to get going. She worried that the admiral might not yet have told patrols there would be a civilian on base, and the fewer men in uniform she had to speak to, the better. It wouldn't be a concern once she received her credentials this afternoon.

She'd need to get over this fear soon if she was going to work on a military base.

After removing the T-shirt and shorts she wore over her swimsuit, Keilani pulled on her wetsuit. At the last second she pulled her Glock from the bag and tucked it safely inside the waterproof barrier of her wetsuit. It shouldn't be left out for anyone to find. She also felt safer with it close by. Some habits were hard to break.

She met the cold waves with a deep breath and began swimming before she could change her mind. When the tide started to pull, she swam with it for a little ways before doubling back toward the shoreline where it ran close to the base. The tide could be dangerous to someone who didn't know what they were doing, and even strong swimmers could get caught up in it, so she kicked harder and hurried her strokes, trying to keep her bearings. It wouldn't do to get lost out here on the day of her arrival.

Diving below the surface, she found what she had hoped for. Slender lines barely disturbing the water indicated the division wall of the dolphin enclosure. She had seen enough of them to recognize it immediately. She emerged from the water to take a breath, and then plunged in deep for a good look.

This time, however, something else caught her eye. Off to her right, two figures in scuba gear were swimming clumsily with what appeared to be a small crate or chest of some sort. Farther out to sea, the shadow of a boat darkened the water. Beyond that, the bay looked deserted. Odd.

Probably time to go before she ended up in trouble somehow. If she had happened onto some kind of top-secret training or something, she could be endangering her job. She hadn't even had a chance to prove her abilities to them yet, and they might not understand her need to get to know her surroundings. She tried to keep her past from affecting her future, but military protocols made her nervous.

Spinning herself around with one leg, Keilani found the other leg caught in a vise-like grip. A swift tug on it plunged her deeper into the blue depths. Panic swamped her. Instinct prompted a gasp, which she barely suppressed in time to avoid drowning. She gave a fierce kick, but the hand barely loosened. Kicking and struggling as hard as she could, Keilani finally managed to break the iron grip. She swam hard, fighting the current all the way back to the break on the beach. She could feel an occasional brush against her bare feet, assuring her she wasn't yet safe. The diver's presence loomed behind her, a silent but very real threat.

Lungs burning, Keilani prayed silently. Whoever pursued her didn't intend to help her to shore; that much she knew. She was thankful for her years of competitive swimming, which had conditioned her to withstand the rigors of this chase. It seemed her pursuer wasn't at all a bad swimmer, either, though. She hadn't gained any significant distance on him.

Finally, a current caught on the edge of the break, pushing her toward shore and her pursuer back out to sea. Breaking the surface, she gulped in air, finally in sight of the shore. She didn't dare take long to rest, however. She dove forward, allowing the waves to help propel her onto the beach, where she stood and began to run.

The sand, thick and damp, sucked at her ankles, slowing her progress, but she fought for speed, muscles burning with every step. Ignoring her discarded belongings, Keilani kept running until she reached the edge of a parking lot near the naval base. At last she turned to look over her shoulder at her pursuer.

He was gone. Facing forward, she heaved in deep

breaths, one after another, until two strong hands clamped onto her arms from behind.

"Who are you and what are you doing here?" A fierce frown was the first thing she noticed about the man.

Keilani tried to lurch back at the gruff question, but the grip held firm. She squirmed, twisting and turning. Ugly memories invaded at the physical contact. The strong hands gave her a little shake.

"Answer me." With that deep voice and confidence, he was probably used to being obeyed immediately.

At last she took a deep breath and really looked at him. He wore a navy uniform and was completely dry. He couldn't possibly have been her pursuer. "M-my name is Keilani. Dr. Keilani Lucas, actually."

He just stared at her, expression hard, waiting for her to continue.

"I'm—I'm the veterinarian and dolphin trainer here as a consultant for the naval marine mammal program." She twisted her shoulders once more. "Please. You're hurting me."

He released her slowly, as if afraid she would run, then frowned. But he didn't apologize.

"You aren't supposed to be here until tomorrow." His steel-gray eyes betrayed nothing.

"I got here a day early and wanted to look around. The admiral gave me permission to explore my new surroundings." She hated the weakness she heard in her own voice.

"By swimming? And running up the beach like you're on fire?" His voice demanded an explanation.

She tried to resist. "Yeah. Sure."

His steely jaw hardened further, lips set in a hard line. "Start talking."

He stepped closer, his sheer size menacing in itself. The breadth of his chest blocked her view of anything beyond him, his height casting a shadow over her.

"I was swimming and someone grabbed me by the ankle. I got scared." It seemed explanation enough, but he wasn't satisfied. The gray eyes narrowed.

"Where were you?"

She pointed vaguely. "Out in that cove."

"Where in the cove? Next to the dolphin enclosure?"

"Not exactly. I didn't get close to it." She had no idea if he would be angry if she had. She didn't want to take that risk.

"Close enough you saw it." It wasn't a question.

She nodded. He saw through her.

"There are no civilians allowed in that area without clearance. Technically, you don't yet have clearance." His expression was as hard as his voice.

Don't look at the uniform.

Keilani took a deep breath. She wasn't going to let him intimidate her—or at least she wouldn't let him know that he did. "I didn't think the area was restricted. It isn't posted, and I was just swimming."

"It is posted." He paused to point, then looked back at her, his expression saying something wasn't right. "Well, it is supposed to be. They must be replacing the signs. But you should have had navy personnel escort you if you wanted to look around. It could be dangerous." His mouth was a hard line. Somehow, he still managed to be handsome.

Keilani just stared back at him, ignoring the salt water tickling down her skin as it dried in the sun. She reached up and twisted her long, dark hair until the water dripped out. Her breathing was still coming fast and hard. Dangerous, yes. She was finding that out.

He huffed out a breath. "I can make things difficult for you if you want. Or you can cooperate."

She looked up at him with a shrug. "With what?"

"Who was chasing you and why? I want details. All of them."

When she remained silent, he reached for her again. "Maybe someone else should have the dolphin trainer consultant position. Let's go have a talk with my commanding officer. Or Admiral McLeary, since you already seem to know him well."

She planted her feet in the sand and glared at him. "I don't know, okay? He was wearing a full wetsuit and scuba gear. And I have no idea why the guy chased me."

He scrutinized her for a moment before nodding. "Then we'd better get you checked in. Someone needs to know you could be in danger." He motioned for her to follow him.

"Can I at least get my belongings? I left them on the beach." She still hadn't moved.

He looked over his shoulder at her. "I'll get them. Where?"

She told him where she had left them and watched him sprint away. He made running through the heavy sand look easy, she noticed. And why didn't he care that it would be all in his shoes?

She kept glancing around her to make sure her attacker didn't return, realizing she didn't even know who this man helping her was. She had intentionally ignored his uniform. She had also been too busy trying not to think about those piercing gray eyes, not to mention the impossibly broad shoulders. She had clearly been without oxygen for too long out there. Why else would she be noticing a man?

When the object of her thoughts came back empty-handed, however, her stomach pulsed in anxiety. "You didn't find my things?"

"The beach is empty." His rigid posture discouraged questions, but she didn't care.

"But I left my clothes and my bag. Are you sure? My phone, my ID, everything was there." She ignored his protest and jogged down the beach.

Fresh panic washed over her as she realized he was right. Her things were gone. She dashed frantically on down the beach, searching, hoping and praying. When she realized the futility of her search, she turned to find he was there.

She put a hand to her head. "I have nothing. I can't even prove to you that I am who I say I am."

He pressed his lips together. "That's easily solved. We already have your identification on file from your application. But if this person was after you for a reason, they now know everything about you."

Micah hadn't needed this kind of trouble today. It was the tenth anniversary of his father's death and he had had hoped to finish his workday early and go home to call his mother. But this wasn't something he could ignore.

He hadn't been able to mentally prepare for Dr. Lucas's arrival, since she hadn't been due to start working until tomorrow. He was honestly irritated that she was coming at all. He had been training the dolphins on his own for over a year and now all of a sudden they wanted to change things on him? He didn't need her help, and it was an insult to his abilities that the admiral had insisted. They had other vets on staff and he didn't need a training consultant. He suspected it was more of a PR stunt than legitimate need. Seeing that she was young and attractive just compounded his irritation, for a plethora of reasons. Mainly because he didn't want a woman in his life and here was a stunningly attractive one, thrown right into his path.

And now she looked frightened and vulnerable—two things he could never ignore. Also two things he had hoped never to encounter in a woman again.

"I'm sorry, but who are you and why are you helping me?" Her forehead creased at her question and it occurred to him he should have told her sooner.

"Lieutenant Micah Kent, head of the naval dolphin training program here in Coronado. We'll be working together in the very near future." He extended a hand.

He had tried to keep his tone neutral, but he could see from her expression that she read his annoyance at the situation. "Oh, I see. Then I'm pleased to meet you."

He nodded, thinking to return the sentiment, but the unexpected ping of a gunshot sent him into action instead. For a split second, his mind returned to that horrible night in Afghanistan when they had been ambushed. The heat and the smell of burnt ammo replayed in his senses.

Keilani cried out, returning his thoughts to the present. How long would he have these flashbacks? He pushed her down, just out of the line of fire as he urged her to run. A trickle of blood ran down her arm from where the bullet had grazed her shoulder. She slapped a hand over it, but kept moving. She didn't even look at the wound.

"Head for that green door on your right." He nudged her in that direction as he pulled his government-issue Sig from his belt. Checking to see that she was following orders this time, he turned and fired in the direction from which the shots had come. More shots flew his way, and he urged Keilani to move faster. Once they reached the door, he checked his gun and grasped his ID card to swipe for clearance.

To his surprise, he heard shots right behind him, and he turned to find Keilani firing her own weapon with precision and confidence. Where had she stashed the Glock? And better yet, why? He blinked as he opened the door while someone let out a grunt in the distance. He'd had no idea she had a weapon hidden away in that wetsuit.

Jerking her inside, he slammed the door behind them. "Nice." He nodded at her.

"What? You expected a panicked damsel?" She dropped the hand holding the gun to her side.

"Yeah, I guess so." He grinned before urging her on. "Come on. We need to file a report."

Another gunshot ricocheted off the door. Her brows rose but he motioned her on.

"You're safe now. They aren't getting through that door." He tried to sound soothing, but judging from the way she winced, it came out as gruff and sharp as everything else he said.

He led her through a long, empty corridor and down a flight of stairs into the basement. When they came to an office with a closed door that had his name on it, he unlocked it and motioned her inside.

"Sit. I've gotta make a couple of calls." He pointed

to a stiff-backed chair before folding himself into his own chair behind the desk.

Keilani did as he suggested, but perched on the edge of her seat. He imagined he could still hear her heart pounding, though her face was pretty calm. Rich brown eyes framed by thick, dark lashes sloped up just slightly; her small, pert nose widening above full red lips. Her appearance certainly fit her name. He could see her on an island surfing or entertaining tourists.

She shivered and he came to his senses.

"Maybe I should see about getting you something dry to wear first." He stood and moved to the door, but stopped and turned back to see if she agreed.

She gave him an appreciative smile and he realized she must have been uncomfortable. He nodded and strode down the hall to a storage closet where he rummaged around until he found something that he thought would fit her. It was an old uniform, but under the circumstances, anything was surely better than the high-necked wetsuit she wore at present. Not that she wasn't absolutely perfect in it, but he definitely had no business noticing when he had no intention of getting involved with anyone. He had learned his lesson. Love was not on his agenda.

She thanked him with a gracious nod when he returned with the clothing and showed her to the ladies' restroom where she could change.

Before she could enter, he motioned to where the blood was drying across the top edge of her shoulder. "Your arm."

"It's just a scratch. I'll clean it up. A small bandage will be sufficient." She seemed more concerned with the nick in her wetsuit than her skin.

He retrieved a square of cotton and some antiseptic from a nearby cupboard for her to treat it with. "Do you need some help?"

She offered him a small smile. "I'm a vet. I think I can manage such a tiny wound."

He nodded, face flushing just a bit. She entered the restroom, and he returned to his desk to call his commanding officer. Captain Jarvis sent him directly to the admiral.

He again explained the situation and that he believed Keilani might have seen something that had somehow put her in danger.

The response wasn't good. "They did what, now? I don't think so. Who's getting past security around my base? Are you pulling my leg, Kent? I'm going to have some heads for this. What happened to these men who were shooting at you? And where is this Dr. Lucas?"

"Sir, she wasn't on base, but just outside on the beach. She's in some kind of trouble. I'm not sure this is going to work." He had explained how he found her and how they had been pursued back to the base. "Maybe we should hold off on her starting here. We could be putting everyone in danger, especially Dr. Lucas."

"Look, I know you haven't wanted her help from the start. But you're going to have to give this a shot. And if some idiot thinks they can get us to back off on this, they might as well forget it. It just confirms to me that we need to do it." The admiral's voice held a note of firm finality. "Meanwhile, you're assigned to protective duty. And I'm going to reassign some men if they can't handle security. I will find out who did this."

"Protective duty? You mean, like her bodyguard? But, sir—"

"No arguments. Keep her safe or it's on your head." The admiral hung up and Micah bit back a sigh. Just what he needed.

"Yes, sir," Micah muttered to the empty room, hanging up the phone. He sat back and let out a sigh of frustration. So there was more to Keilani's hire than PR and publicity, just as he had suspected. The admiral didn't seem surprised by what Keilani had seen. Unfortunately, he knew the admiral well enough to know he would never explain what was going on until he was ready.

TWO

Keilani stared into the mirror. She wouldn't give in to the physical shock. She knew the signs. She inhaled deeply and counted, clearing her mind, thinking of blue skies, fluffy clouds and sunshine. When she opened them again, she saw a stranger in a female naval officer's uniform—a stranger with her eyes.

Had she been wrong to accept this job? Her instincts said no, but her mind was beginning to grow concerned that she had made the wrong decision. Between the events of the afternoon and the introduction to the entirely too attractive new coworker, she was in complete turmoil. And she hadn't even begun her job yet.

Wiping her salty cheeks with a wet paper towel, she decided to face whatever was next head-on. She had no excuse to cower in the ladies' room. She had overcome far worse circumstances in her life. A prayer for strength whispered across her lips, one that had become as familiar as her own skin over the years. Peace filled her. She wasn't alone in this.

She returned to Lieutenant Kent's office to find him on the phone. She tried to duck out to wait in the corridor until he finished, but he motioned her inside. While he continued his conversation, she took the opportunity to observe him freely. His dark hair had the slightest wave, cut short and a little messy. His eyes were a gunmetal gray with just the slightest hint of blue when the light hit them, and his strong jaw accented full lips that stood out in the midst of his stubble. Though he had the hard look of a navy SEAL, there was a certain indefinable quality about him that made him…different.

Stop noticing. You don't exactly have a good track record with men, Keilani silently reprimanded herself. She decided long ago she was better off independent. There was no need for a man in her life. Her past experience was more than she needed.

"I appreciate it, sir. We will get her situated." When Micah had disconnected, he fixed Keilani with a dark look. Even that didn't convince her he was as tough as he appeared. Physically, maybe, but that was it.

"Something else is wrong." Her voice was whisper quiet in the silent room.

"That was Captain Jarvis. But I also spoke to the admiral and it looks like you're going to be stuck with me until we figure this out." His tone was neutral, but his eyes searched hers. What did he expect to find? Protest? Anger? Or something more personal?

She focused on revealing nothing. "What does that mean?"

"It means I'm assigned to protect you until we know you're safe. You'll be bunking at my place and I'll go with you everywhere but the ladies' room." He stared hard at her. "Are you sure there's nothing else you can tell me about what you saw?"

She could sense that he was asking for more than one reason. He clearly felt uncomfortable having protective responsibility for her. But why? He seemed perfectly capable.

He tapped a pencil against the calendar square on top of his desk, his veins standing up in blue-green lines across the top of his tanned hand. She realized he was watching her study him, and heat flowed up into her cheeks.

Turning her gaze instead to her surroundings, Keilani realized his office space was practically empty except for the most basic of necessities. The navy's requirement, or Micah's choice? And what did it say about him?

She returned her focus to the question she had almost forgotten about.

"Would it change anything?" Keilani didn't want to be chained to him any more than he wanted to be stuck with her. She began to squirm. When he lifted one eyebrow, she knew he noticed.

She decided full disclosure was in their best interest. "Should there be men…um, with crates, out in the bay? Just beyond the dolphin enclosure?"

She still wasn't sure telling him was her best idea. His expression was still frightening and he might not appreciate her interference. In her experience, men usually preferred women to ask for permission, defer to their opinions, and mind their own business. She wasn't exactly starting off making the best impression on her new coworker.

Lieutenant Kent leaned forward, shaking his head. "Men with crates? Why don't you start at the beginning?"

His eyes filled with a new emotion, something like interest, or maybe irritation? She didn't have any way of knowing for sure this man wasn't going to be angry with her for what she had seen. But she didn't think he was involved in whatever had been happening in the bay or else he would have retaliated before now, and besides, she had already mentioned what she knew. Her hands shook as she looped her fingers together.

Keilani inhaled some courage and settled her hands in her lap. She began to explain to him about her exploratory swim, leaving out the part about her nerves. She told him about the boat and how she had believed it to be affiliated with the navy, and then how someone had grabbed her ankle and tried to pull her farther under, pursuing her back to the beach.

His expression had been darkening steadily as she told her story. It made her shudder, remembering a time she had seen another man's expression go dark.

Finally, he spoke. "Yet you escaped? You swam all that way with someone pursuing you and had the stamina left to run all the way up that beach? That's pretty impressive."

She stiffened. "Don't patronize me. I know how rigorous SEAL training is."

He stared her down, making her want to squirm once more. "I wasn't. That's a tough swim. As a SEAL, I should know."

Keilani watched him for a long moment. Respect flickered in his eyes. "I used to compete in long-distance swimming and surfing."

He nodded. "Nice. Why did you stop?"

She debated for a moment, but settled on a vague answer. "Family reasons."

She sensed his displeasure, though his expression did little to reveal it. He didn't push for more. "I see."

If he had any thoughts on the boat and the men with the crates, he refrained from sharing them with her. "I

have a few other things to take care of, but if you can
wait here, we'll go get whatever you need to relocate."

She nodded, but couldn't avoid asking the question
that was burning in her thoughts.

"Do you live alone?" The idea of being alone in a
house with this man made her nervous for more reasons than one.

"No. You'll meet Xavier and Emmett tonight. There's
plenty of room at our place and you'll be well protected." He stood, so she followed suit.

"That isn't necessary. I have already signed a lease
on a small apartment. It's gated and secure." It was far
too personal, too intimate, to sleep in his house, considering they had just met. And with her past, she didn't
warm up to strange men easily.

"Absolutely not. I was assigned protective duty over
you, and you will have it 24/7." He offered her a slight,
crooked grin—the first thing resembling a smile she
had seen on his face—and her breath caught. It was
definitely going to be a rough few days under his close
scrutiny.

"I don't suppose I have any input, then." Her voice
sounded breathy and she cleared her throat and turned
away. The last thing she wanted him thinking was that
she was some infatuated girl he could twist around his
finger. Men in uniform tended to enjoy having that effect on women, in her experience. *Get a grip, sister.*

"How about I introduce you to a few of the dolphins
we will be working with first?" He held the door open
and waited. Could he tell she was struggling, her nerves
crumpling under the pressure? He seemed to want to
make this easier for her. Why? What could he possibly have to gain from doing so? In her experience, men

only showed concern and caring when they had some interest in the outcome.

Whatever it was, all she could do was accept it right now. She turned back to him, relieved to have a distraction. The thought of her career, her passion, chased all the anxiety away. From his expression, she could tell he felt something a little like relief as well, and maybe even a little bit of pleasure. Maybe if she spent more time in his company, she could relax about accepting his protection. And it wasn't as if she had a choice.

She nodded, smiling with her eyes. "I'd like that very much. Thank you."

The naval dolphin enclosure was much different from the other training facilities she had worked in. There were similarities, of course, but this one was clearly designed for functionality rather than aesthetics. Just like everything else she had encountered on base so far, it was high-tech, functional and secure. It was situated on the edge of the naval base with a maze of dolphin pens stretching out toward the ocean. Several of the pens reached far into the bay and grew larger the farther out they went. It created a massive rectangle of divided enclosures. Surprisingly, it was open to the outside so she could only assume it was well-patrolled by the navy. Down the middle was an alleyway leading into the training area.

Micah, as he had insisted she call him, showed her every last detail of the facilities. There was even a miniature veterinary hospital situated on one end equipped with nearly anything one might need to treat a sick or injured cetacean. Judging by the amount of pride he took in the enclosure, she could only assume Micah must have a personal connection to the design of it somehow.

"And now let's meet the real superstars." He pushed a button on a control panel and an underwater door lifted. He leaned into a tank and gave a signal. Two sleek bodies sluiced through the water toward them at lightning speed. Two more soon followed, and at another signal from Micah, they broke the surface with their smooth bottle noses, and began to chitter at them gleefully. He rewarded the dolphins and began the introductions. The crinkles at the corners of his eyes as he pointed each of them out were a testament to how he felt about the creatures.

"This dainty thing here is Nikita. The husky girl here is Mulan. Stefan and Rambo are the two gentlemen. They are just slow, not polite. The ladies beat them at nearly everything except devouring their dinner. Say hello to Keilani, kids." At his signal they waved with one fin before chittering at them again.

"My, my. They are superstars." Keilani offered them a friendly greeting. "Real beauties, too. Some of the finest dolphins I've seen."

Micah's expression didn't change, but his chest seemed to expand just a bit. "Only the finest for the navy SEALs."

"I'm stoked about the job, honestly. It's so much more meaningful than some of the positions I've held in the past. I love working with dolphins, but theme park entertainment hardly compares with national security." Keilani watched as the small pod swam away at Micah's dismissal command. Though navy dolphins had many jobs, such as bomb detection and identifying and warning SEALs of the presence of enemy swimmers, they were also well trained in obedience so they wouldn't get lost on missions.

"We have plans for expansion. These are just our top agents right now. We have several more, and some of the females are expecting." He led her into another section of the facility. "Some are this way. Of course, not all of our dolphins are housed together. For security reasons."

"This is amazing," Keilani said, looking around the elaborate expanse of pools.

"We work on improvements for them every day. That's why you're here, of course. They are part of the family. Not every dolphin is qualified to be a part of our SEAL team. So some are released, if it's safe for them, or sometimes they are transported to a civilian facility."

They walked through yards and yards of pathways along the massive enclosures. "This is a major opera-tion." Keilani knew her mouth must be open in awe, but she couldn't contain her excitement.

"It's pretty big." He showed her the way back into the base and told her more about the program. Return-ing to his office, he explained the files they kept on all of the dolphins. They had thorough records for every cetacean on the grounds, whether they were born in captivity or brought in from the ocean. He offered her a few of the files to look at while he completed his own tasks, asking her to review the findings on the health of the dolphins in question. Occasionally, they had some issues with illness, and though the veterinarians in naval employ were very good, he said he liked to make sure that everything was up to standards.

There was a definite tension in the room. Keilani watched him through lowered lashes and found he was also glancing at her even as he worked on the tasks before him. Was her presence a distraction to him? The thought made her uncomfortable. She didn't want to keep him from his work. She considered excusing herself, but she didn't know where else to go.

Eventually, he completed his tasks, and when he stood to go, Keilani stood, as well. She handed him the files and he put them back in the cabinet.

"Let's get something to eat, and then we'll go get you settled." Keilani wasn't really hungry, but she also wasn't ready for him to take her back to his house. It seemed really awkward in every way. They knew practically nothing about one another, but they would be stuck with each other indefinitely. It was a strange way to begin their working relationship. She didn't care for it at all.

They were walking out when one of his team members nearly ran into them. "Oh, sorry, Lieutenant Kent." The man saluted before eyeing Keilani carefully.

"Petty Officer Dalton Taggert, I'd like to introduce you to Dr. Keilani Lucas. She's the civilian consultant for the marine mammal program. She just arrived, but you'll be seeing her around base."

Something flashed across the man's expression briefly, but it was gone so quickly she decided she had imagined it. Taggert smiled and extended a hand to Keilani. "It's great to meet you. Someone certainly needs to get Lieutenant Kent in line."

She glanced at Micah to confirm the man was teasing, and he gave her an inconspicuous nod to confirm it. She smiled back at Taggert. "I'll do my best."

She noticed the officer watched Micah for a moment, his smile fading, but then gave her another nod before leaving.

As Taggert moved away, Micah extended a hand. "After you, Dr. Lucas."

The bistro on the corner seemed like a quiet enough place for them to have some lunch and the waiter graciously settled them at a shady outdoor table with a nice view. Micah explained that he liked being able to see most of the people coming and going around the corner. It made him feel more secure.

Keilani made small talk about the dolphins and Micah responded with brief comments, seemingly consumed with his thoughts, until she mentioned her reason for coming.

"I know the navy said a part of this job would be to mend the reputation of the marine mammal program because there have been some nasty articles circulating about the treatment of your animals. I've read many of them, but I'll admit, I'm not sure why there has been much credence given to them. Is there something else I should know?"

Micah tilted his water glass, watching the liquid tilt, as well. "You know as much as I do. I suspect there might be more to the navy's reasons for bringing you here, but if there is, it's information I'm not privy to. I suppose we'll find out together."

She pressed her lips into a thin line. "I see. So you think the admiral hiring me is just a front for something?" She honestly couldn't understand why the navy needed an outside consultant now when they hadn't used one before.

He gazed up at her, a penetrating look pinning her to her spot from across the table. "Possibly. But it doesn't make sense. I really think it would be in everyone's best interest to know what the mission is, if possible.

But there is no understanding the reasoning of the US Navy."

"I guess I should be prepared for anything, then." She tried to sound unconcerned, but the idea made her nervous. Feeling self-conscious, she scanned around for something to distract them.

"Isn't that how life always is?" He said it lightly, but she thought he might be feeling some tension, as well. His jaw seemed tightly clenched. His long fingers toyed with a napkin.

It had been a long time since she had eaten a meal with a man in this type of atmosphere. She hadn't dated anyone since the terrible breakup with Jackson. She hadn't wanted to. Even now, knowing it wasn't a date, being alone with a man made her nervous.

They didn't discuss it any more over the food, instead keeping to topics such as the local climate and their mutual interest in dolphin care and training techniques. She felt a little more relaxed by the time they paid the tab and prepared to leave. From his mannerisms, Keilani thought Micah almost relaxed, too.

Almost.

A man like Micah Kent never completely relaxed.

They had to go inside to pay, and when they had finished, Micah led her out through a door that overlooked the bay. They'd just headed down the empty beach where the sun hung like a glowing bulb over the horizon when the beautiful illusion of peace was shattered.

Keilani felt a tingle race up her spine about the same time Micah shoved her to the ground. A shot rang out and the hard red line of a laser sight danced around, trying to relocate its target. Her pulse thundered in her ears and she could taste the salt in the sea air. All her senses seemed heightened. Her throat tightened and she felt the pressure of Micah's weight easing off her as she noted the smell of gunpowder.

"Run!" Micah helped her to her feet as he shouted the order.

Keilani rose just enough to allow the efficiency of movement she needed, but soon another shot pinged close by. She stayed low and followed Micah's direction with no idea where she was headed. How could they have known where to look for her?

She glanced back to see if Micah still followed her just in time to watch him go down as a stark red blossom of blood stained the side of his uniform.

A scream tried to rip from her throat, but she squelched it, only a yelp emerging. Micah looked up at her and waved her on. He was still alive, at least.

He crawled after her, she noted at next glance, then he barked at her to move. Another bullet pinged, proving that the sniper was a professional. He wasted no time reloading. To her amazement, Micah was on his feet—pale, but determined. He didn't let her get too far ahead of him before catching up.

They had emerged on the far end of the café where there was very little available to them in the way of shields. Her back ached from the strain, but the intermittent dinging of bullets urged her on. She felt the slight pressure of Micah's hand there, also. The shots seemed to grow closer, the shrapnel from where the bullets were striking the concrete grazing the backs of their legs.

Keilani watched as Micah scanned the area, probably looking for any sort of cover between them and the navy side of the beach. The street was on the other side of the building. Micah gestured for her to follow, then made for some docks down the pier. Was he hoping the shooter would lose them in the maze of vessels and boat slips?

The shots coming from the sniper didn't slow down any, though. Every time they emerged from cover of any sort, another bullet whizzed toward them. They ducked and darted, unable to stay out of sight for long. Keilani's nerves were completely frazzled.

They reached the end of the pier and found they were out of options. Micah slid to a halt and fixed his gaze on her. She didn't like the look he was giving her, not at all.

"I'm sorry, Keilani." He sucked in a breath and pointed at a broad expanse of water to her left. "We're going to have to swim for it."

Keilani was more than prepared to comply with his command. The sniper fire seemed unending and she was desperate to make it stop. The wool fabric of the uniform was heavy as she dove into the briny water, but she managed to make decent time. She didn't dare surface, but Micah's presence was sure behind her. He overtook her and led the way, swimming below the surface until Keilani thought her lungs would burst. Her eyes stung from the bite of the salt and she ached with fatigue.

They swam for what seemed like forever before she noticed the changes in the water that indicated they were nearing the dolphin enclosures. Micah kept below the surface for long periods of time before coming up to breathe and she was beginning to tire.

From the shadows above them she assumed they were heading through the tunnels back toward the indoor pools where trainers worked with the cetaceans. She hadn't realized they could reach the enclosures from the far side of the bay, but she was thankful. The beach must have just been on the other side of the bay where it curved around the naval base. She was still pretty unfamiliar with the layout of the Coronado area.

A few curious dolphins watched them swim past from their glassed-in pens, and a couple even followed them down the lanes with their eyes, anxious to join whatever game the humans were playing. Keilani hoped the water would stop any stray bullets from reaching the innocent dolphins, if indeed the sniper still had eyes on them. He should have lost them while they were underwater.

Micah swam ahead of her, and she was impressed with his speed. She hadn't realized she had fallen so far behind, but when a gate slammed closed just in front of her, she almost smacked into it. Looking up, she realized she was underground. Panic filled her. Behind her was an unknown enemy and she was trapped in a tunnel with nowhere to go and no air to breathe.

Her mind conjured up images of being shut in that small, dark room from her childhood with hardly any air, her stepfather laughing cruelly from the other side. The sound of the key turning in the lock, the finality of his footsteps walking away. Fear bubbled up inside her in waves.

She tried banging on the gate, but the sound was muffled under the water. She tried harder, wondering how long it would be before Micah realized she wasn't right behind him. Would she drown before he found her? She tried again with as much force as she could manage against the drag from the water. Her air was running out quickly.

She fought for calm. Panicking would only make it worse. It was hard to relax when she couldn't take deep breaths, though. She felt herself losing consciousness just before she realized Micah was turning around to look for her.

He hurried back to the gate, pushing on it with all his strength. Thankfully, it somehow gave way and Micah broke through. He tugged at her listless hand, pulling her toward the surface just outside the tunnel, and she struggled to follow him up out of the water. She broke the surface, gasping from adrenaline as well as oxygen deprivation. The fire in her lungs came close to choking her. She barely had the strength to keep her head above water. Micah had to help her from the pool.

"It's a good thing you're a strong swimmer. Are you okay?" Micah's deep voice broke the eerie silence. A door slammed somewhere and Keilani jumped, almost tumbling back into the water. Micah steadied her with a hand at her lower back. Her eyes shot to his, the adrenaline of fear quickly replaced by something she didn't know how to identify. It made her nervous. She wanted rid of it.

She could only assume he felt it, too, when he smiled roguishly at her. "So much for your dry clothes."

Keilani didn't respond right away. She was all too aware of the precarious predicament she was in, but it didn't inhibit the other unwelcome feelings coursing through her. "I think I've done enough swimming for the day."

The corners of his mouth turned down at her falsely

bright tone. Before he could comment, however, another officer burst into the enclosure.

"Lieutenant Kent! What are you doing here? I thought you were gone for the day."

"It wasn't exactly a choice. Why are you here?" Micah frowned at the other man.

"I heard voices in here and I had heard from the CO there was some trouble with the dolphin trainer earlier. I thought I had better check it out, just in case." The man looked genuinely concerned.

Micah shucked his dripping jacket. His shirt sleeve was stained with blood that looked like a watercolor paint accident. He looked at Keilani, who was watching him with a concerned expression.

"Can I help?" Keilani asked. "You need to treat that wound right away."

"I can handle it. But we need to go speak to the admiral about this as soon as possible. Taggert, would you let him know we are coming?"

The man agreed to do as Micah asked and left.

"So we are going back to the admiral's office?" Keilani didn't look too happy about that.

He pulled some gauze and tape from a cabinet in the room and began to treat the open wound where the bullet had grazed his flesh. His gritted teeth attested to the self-control it took to hold it together as he strained to doctor his own wound. Without asking again, Keilani began to help him.

"Yeah, I'm afraid so." He winced as she bandaged the stinging wound. "I sure hope he has a solution."

Whatever Micah had expected from Dr. Keilani Lucas before her arrival, this wasn't it. She was throwing him completely off his game. Her physical and mental strength alone made him stand back and stare, and the woman herself just had him in awe. As trite as it sounded to his own ears, he had never met anyone like her.

He couldn't deny that he was beginning to feel an attachment to her. She had a strength of character he wouldn't have expected. And if the way she responded to him was any indication, she felt the same way. But he didn't have plans to form any romantic attachments—now or ever. That meant he had to keep his distance, despite any feelings he might have. After being betrayed by Jade, he didn't want to take the chance again. She had shown him just how one-sided love could be.

As they walked to the admiral's quarters, however, his curiosity got the better of him. "Where did you learn to handle a gun? I never got the chance to ask you earlier."

She frowned. "My grandfather taught me."

He wasn't satisfied with this, nor was he going to let it go at that. "Why your grandfather?"

She shrugged. "We were close. He thought I should be able to defend myself."

"In general, or for some specific reason?" Thoughts of a violent boyfriend in her past made him angry on her behalf. It happened far too often. Was that why she had learned to shoot?

She seemed to be considering her answer, because she didn't speak for several seconds. "Both, I guess. It's rather personal."

He was confounded by her vague answer, but he also felt certain she had no intention of telling him the details. He couldn't really blame her. He probably wouldn't share such intimate details of his life with her right now, either.

"Well, I'm glad someone taught you. I just wish you'd never had to use that particular skill." He opened a door for her and waited while she passed into the new corridor.

"I've had to use a lot of skills since arriving in California this morning that I hoped not to need. It's so much different from island life in Hawaii." Her wry smile made him lift one corner of his own mouth.

"I imagine so. I'm sorry you've had such a lousy welcome." He kept his eyes on the corridor in front of him until he felt her watching him, and then he turned his head slowly to look at her.

Keilani's luminous eyes were all seriousness now. "I owe you a lot of thanks. If not for your help…"

When she let it trail off, he shook his head. "I'd do it all again. And you would have made it, somehow. I don't know you that well, but I can already guess you would have found a way."

He realized they had both stopped and stood staring at each other in the corridor, until the officer stuck his head out a nearby door to see where they were. The moment was broken and Keilani looked away. He didn't completely let it go, though. He leaned close to her ear and whispered, "You're welcome."

Keilani blushed as she walked into the admiral's quarters.

THREE

Keilani fought the urge to put her head in her hands. It felt like she had answered the same questions at least a dozen times. Admiral McLeary was almost terrifying, especially considering her phobia of rigid uniforms. He had brusquely ordered someone to provide a towel for her, but made no other concessions for her comfort. Micah, too, stood dripping at attention beside her chair. The admiral hadn't even acknowledged him, but neither had he dismissed him.

At last, Micah requested permission to speak.

"What is it, Lieutenant?"

"With all due respect, sir, I think Keilani is a bit overwhelmed. This might be more productive once she's had some time to recover from the day's events." Micah didn't glance her way, but the admiral fixed her with a stare.

Finally, his hard expression softened a bit. "You might be right. If you'll excuse me, ma'am, I'm accustomed to working with the toughest military men in the country." He glanced at Micah. "I think she can hold her own, though."

"Pardon, sir, but I'm confident she can. But if we're dismissed—"

"Not just yet. Part of the reason I asked Dr. Lucas to join us is to assist you with a big job. I want you to identify a new type of system that local drug smugglers are using in our area. It's affecting our operations and I want to put a stop to it ASAP."

"What exactly is it we are looking for, sir?" Micah's teeth were clenched. What was he stressed about?

"If I knew, I wouldn't be putting such priority on it. The rumors say it is passing through every security measure undetected and I want to know how. Figure it out. Train the dolphins to find drugs. Whatever it is you need to complete that task, let me know. I'll be waiting for updates."

Micah nodded and began to stand.

"One more thing." The admiral held up a hand. "I'm closing down all access to the dolphin enclosures."

"But sir, we—"

"Not to you and Dr. Lucas. But no one else will be allowed within a hundred feet without my personal permission. I'll post additional guards on all sides to enforce it. But I want you to get started tomorrow." The admiral stood. "You're dismissed."

Micah led Keilani out of the office and down the corridor. When he took her out the door and to a black Nissan Titan in the parking lot, she finally asked her burning question.

"Where are we going?"

"First to get your things." He held the door open on the passenger side.

She hesitated a moment before climbing in. "And then?"

"And then we'll get you settled and get started." He closed the door before she could respond.

Her heart rate kicked up a notch at the idea of *getting settled* at Micah's place. She watched him walk around the front of the truck, his gait a combination of ease and raw masculine power. It wasn't going to be an option to avoid noticing him. She was going to have to toughen up.

The truck seemed entirely too small with Keilani's presence alongside him. Her fidgeting was distracting, but it was more than that. He couldn't ignore her. He had also noticed she was staring at the admiral's uniform earlier. It had seemed odd that she had fixated on it throughout their discussion.

But he put those thoughts aside for now. He wished he could do the same with the distraction of her presence. Micah's training urged him to put some distance between them. She was a threat. He could feel it as sure as he had felt the enemy's presence overseas before the attack. But his orders were in direct contradiction to what he wanted to do—run.

His wound throbbed, though he had already made a quick assessment and deemed it insignificant. The bullet had grazed the skin of his upper arm near the shoulder, tearing open the flesh. It burned, but it wasn't painful enough to take his mind off things. For once, the training that helped him forget about physical discomfort was a disadvantage. He'd have welcomed a distraction from the woman beside him.

He hoped Keilani wouldn't ask questions about their mission, but he really didn't know enough details to fully explain to her what was going on. If she knew how little he understood about what was happening, would she feel even more frightened than she already was? If so, she might give up on the job before it was even started. And he still wasn't sure if this whole experiment—bringing a civilian in to help with the dolphins—was for the benefit of the public or the navy, or possibly both. The admiral had just convoluted the situation. The dolphins were well equipped to find drugs. It wouldn't take any additional complicated training for them to handle the task. Was there something else going on?

It was odd that someone would be bold enough to smuggle drugs right under their noses, and it seemed a strange coincidence that Keilani was here to help with the dolphins' increased training for drug smuggling prevention and encountered what he was sure was that very thing on her first day. But the investigation team was refusing to disclose anything to him right now other than what they believed was absolutely necessary. He was frustrated by the slow process, but mostly because he wanted to be sure his dolphins were safe.

Keilani was every kind of contradiction he could think of right now, also. She seemed fragile, but expressed a toughness he didn't expect. She was young and beautiful, but her résumé provided an impressive list of skills and experiences. She had every reason to be bold and confident, yet she was quiet and unobtrusive in her manner. He didn't quite know what to do with all of this information, so he just stored it away.

More important, he needed to keep tabs on their surroundings. No one around them had behaved suspiciously as they left, but it was essential to keep watch in a situation like this. He decided to phone ahead to prepare his roomies for what was happening. Emmett answered his phone on the second ring.

"What's up, bro?" Typical Emmett.

"Just a heads-up on a situation we've got going on." Micah explained the day's events as succinctly as he could. "Just need you and Xavier to keep your eyes peeled for anything unusual. Will you tell him?"

"Uh, he's already gone. I can tell him, but you might want to just call him." Emmett explained Xavier's plans to complete a report he had coming due on a recent assignment. "Sorry I missed all the fun, though. See you when you get here."

"Okay. It's no problem. I'll talk to you later, man." Once Micah had disconnected, he did a more thorough search of the mirrors he had been watching the whole time.

Things were quiet. Micah didn't like quiet. It always led to something, and he didn't like waiting, either.

Keilani, too, seemed to be on edge. She said nothing as they drove, only stared out the front windshield as if her thoughts were somewhere else. Micah didn't have that luxury.

Once Micah had taken care of all the details, he concentrated on getting Keilani's things. Her car was parked a few blocks from the base where she had left it before her swim. They were just easing into the parking lot when Micah's senses began to prickle with awareness. SEAL senses, they sometimes called them.

"Stay in the truck no matter what. Lock the doors." Micah barked the order at Keilani as he opened his door. He ignored her surprised expression. A quick scan proved the threat was out of sight, but it didn't matter. It was still there.

He stayed low, prepared to dive for cover if the danger manifested, half jogging between the vehicles in his search. He had silently pulled his Sig and held it at the ready.

He traveled stealthily up and down the parking lot, but there was no one there. Just to be certain, he made another pass and scanned all the nearby rooftops. He finally decided it was something else.

He knew better than to disregard his instincts, so he tapped on the truck window. "Stay there, but unlock your car. I'll get your things."

Keilani nodded and fumbled for her keys, which she must have tucked into her wetsuit with her Glock earlier. She hit the button on her key fob and just as Micah was about to step around the front of the truck and approach her Honda, an explosion rent the air.

Throwing himself to the ground, Micah instantly made his evaluation. The lock switch on her car had been set to trigger a bomb, on a slight delay, that would have blasted her to the next county had she been about to get in it. Fragments of what was once her Honda littered the ground around him, some of them still flaming brightly. He thought Keilani might have screamed, but his focus was elsewhere. He made his way back around to the driver's-side door of his truck and jumped in just as she was about to get out.

"Are you okay?" Keilani asked, releasing the door handle.

He only nodded and threw the truck into Drive. She was examining him from head to toe as if sure he was lying.

"Really, I'm good. We have to get out of here, though.

The perp will be coming to see if the job is done." The tires squalled as he pulled away.

As if in answer, more tires squalled as a black van sped toward them.

"Too late." Keilani cringed and fell down into the seat as Micah whirled the truck around and toward the road.

"Just hold on." Micah gunned it out of the lot, looking for obstacles to put between them and the shooter. A parade of multistoried buildings provided an alley to his left. It seemed his only option.

"Stay down, just in case," he said when he noticed Keilani trying to get a look.

She did as he asked, but her slumped form betrayed her frustration. The metallic ding of a bullet hitting the truck assured them it was a good precaution.

"I'll let you know if anything good happens." He winked at her.

She jumped and made a small shriek as a bullet cracked the windshield. She was making it difficult for him to concentrate on keeping them on the road. When she looked up at him, she seemed even more frightened. He had been told he looked kind of scary when he got in the zone, but this was the first time he believed it.

Focus, Kent. Focus.

Everything in him wanted to charge toward their pursuer and end the danger for good, but with Keilani to protect, that wasn't an option. Her petite form folded up below the dash served as a reminder for him of why he chose this job.

Skidding into the alley, Micah increased his speed again, hoping to spot a new defense option when they came out the other side. From what he could gather, there were two men—one driving and one shooting. He was going to have to think fast. The farther east they traveled, the greater the chance of more civilians getting caught in the crossfire.

He made a gutsy decision.

Slamming on the brakes, Micah sent the truck sliding up next to a curb outside a bank. He took out a dumpster along the curb to make room. Keilani's seatbelt caught, but she was ready, hanging on to the handle at the top of the cab. The shots had slowed, making him suspicious. He needed to act quickly. He pointed. "Keilani, get inside that bank and run to Eli Colby's office, first door on the right. Give him my name and Code 724. He'll lock you in the vault. Go!"

"What?" Her response was a squeak. He would have thought he asked her to crawl into a pit of vipers from the terrified look on her face.

"Just do it. I'll explain later." He had his Sig at the ready, knowing the black van would round the corner any second now. He watched her, ready to do whatever it took to catch the attention of the driver in hopes of drawing fire away from Keilani.

He let out a relieved sigh when she obeyed, then rushed back down the sidewalk in the direction from which they came. When the van turned the corner, he was ready.

Two quick shots blew out both of the driver's-side tires. Micah ducked behind a car when the shooter returned fire. Sirens in the distance assured him Keilani had made it safely into the bank vault. It also informed the men in the van they were out of time.

Two men in jeans and plain T-shirts fled the disabled van, ski masks over their faces, one still shooting in Micah's general direction. He quickly responded by winging the shooter in the firing arm—which Micah noticed was his left.

The men were nearly out of range, so Micah opted to conserve rounds, considering he had no more cartridges in the truck. He would remedy that ASAP.

A quick discussion with an officer sent two in search of the fleeing men, but Micah didn't expect them to be apprehended. As soon as he could get away, he sprinted back to the Federal Reserve Bank.

Keilani was fuming. "Why did you do that? The man shoved me into the vault like a condemned prisoner. He didn't even let me finish telling him what happened."

"Good. He did his job." Micah knew his expression hadn't softened any. He pointed her to the door.

"What exactly is his job?" It was obvious she had no intention of letting it go that easily.

He held open the door to the bank as she stepped outside. "With the naval base and the presence of the SEALs, the trained dolphins and other security issues, we have contacts around the area in case of dangerous situations. The bank, having a secure vault, is an obvious choice."

He had given no consideration to her feelings on being stuffed into the vault. It made her feel a little uneasy. "What if I was claustrophobic? And it kind of scared me being manhandled that way."

So that was it. She didn't like tight spaces.

He looked her over. "You seem to be fine."

Micah didn't miss the mutinous expression that met his grin as she took off for the truck.

He thought she was muttering under her breath. She

was going to be even more unhappy in a moment. "We aren't taking the truck."

She halted. "What? Why not?"

He shrugged. "Protocol. We'll walk to meet my roommate, Emmett, then we'll get another vehicle." He glanced at the once-shiny truck now riddled with bullet holes, the front end smashed from moving the dumpster out of the way. "I'm not especially happy with the condition of my truck right now, either."

She winced. "I'm so sorry. I can pay for repairs."

He let out an incredulous laugh. "No. Besides, I think it's totaled."

It was obvious she felt terrible about it, but he had no idea what to say to her to make it better, so he said nothing.

"Will your insurance go up?" Her eyebrows crinkled together.

He just shook his head. "I'm a SEAL. That's not even an issue."

She clearly didn't understand, but he couldn't take the time to explain it to her right now.

"We have special allowances for things like that. It's sort of a benefit. Our auto insurance is covered through the navy."

People were beginning to look in their direction, curious over recent events, and he could see them putting the pieces together in their minds.

"Keilani, we have to get going."

It took another second or two, but she finally started moving. He couldn't really blame her. She had been through a lot in one day.

"We're going to get you settled and safe." He hoped the quiet promise wouldn't prove to be false.

"I'm fine."

Her body language said otherwise.

Having Emmett with them proved to be a big help with perspective. He had some angles Micah hadn't thought of just yet. They took Emmett's Jeep back to their house to the tune of a million questions.

"Dude, how'd you tear up your arm? You gonna be good to swim? 'Cause I could work with Keilani." He added a few more comments, but Micah never got past that one.

"Emmett, you know next to nothing about the dolphins." In other words, back off.

"I've been thinking I'd like to learn. Maybe she could teach me some things. You could use a hand, right, O Great Dolphin Master? It might come in handy on missions. Wouldn't you want my help, Dr. Lucas?"

Emmett was deliberately refusing to take the hint. "Funny. And it's not a good time. My arm is fine. It's not deep. Keilani and I can handle things."

"But you shouldn't get to have all the fun. Besides, with your aversion to commitment you probably won't do the same job forever, right? Someone will need to take over for you eventually." Emmett kept looking at Keilani, probably trying to gauge her reaction to his remarks.

Now Emmett was just playing dirty by reminding him of his determination to remain single while letting Keilani know he was emotionally unavailable. But he wasn't having it.

"That doesn't mean I want you to move in and try to take my job." *I saw her first.* It was juvenile, but there it was.

Emmett laughed and thumped the steering wheel before throwing up his hands. "All right, fine. So you're a little attached to your dolphins. I guess you're allowed to change your mind. I'll leave it alone."

Uh-oh. He had played right into Emmett's hands. Rookie mistake. Emmett knew exactly where Micah stood with Keilani now. He would be sure to read too much into it. Micah would never hear the end of it.

If he were to be honest, Micah really didn't know where he stood with his feelings about Keilani. He probably felt more tenderness toward her than he would have liked. But with his dangerous career, any relationships were out of the question. She was his responsibility for now, and he didn't want Emmett making things more difficult for her. His friend had a tendency to take things lightly and Micah needed to set up a boundary. The last thing Keilani needed was the worry of someone being too friendly with her while she was in serious danger.

Keilani, however, seemed to be oblivious to the double meanings hiding in the conversation between the two men. He was thankful for that. But she also looked exhausted and that angered him. He felt the deep frown cutting into his face.

"Hey, Emmett, we've got to do some research on these activities in the bay tonight. Do you think you could do some scouting for us?"

"You mean off duty?" He looked a little dubious. "I could try. I have that thing with Hudson, but after that, maybe?"

"Good. Don't mention it to anyone. Not even Hudson." He also glanced at Keilani, who understood and nodded.

"You think they have an inside?" Emmett looked pretty angry at the suggestion.

"I sure hope not. I can't think of anything worse. And besides, who could it be? We're brothers, all of us. No one on the team would betray the rest of us like that." Micah hated the prickling of doubt that he felt. But it was there. He couldn't ignore it.

"You're right. It couldn't be." Emmett shook his head and offered a jovial grin to them both.

When they rolled up to the house, everything looked peaceful. Micah was thankful for that, at least. He showed Keilani to her room, gave her a pair of his shorts and a T-shirt, then offered her his shower. Her grateful expression was all the thanks he needed.

He moved to the living room and sat for a moment with Emmett to drink some coffee. It didn't have much effect on him anymore, but he still drank it, mostly out of habit. Maybe it would speed up his thought processes. Besides, he wouldn't be able to settle down to sleep any time soon.

"She's pretty good-looking." Emmett had at least waited for Keilani to get in the shower before making the comment. "Must be a real trial to be forced to work with her for the next several weeks."

Micah narrowed his eyes. "That's totally irrelevant."

"Not really. She's single. I'm not as phobic of commitment as you are. She won't be in danger forever. I mean, maybe I could even volunteer to protect her and get you off the hook. You could concentrate on the dolphins." Emmett played it off, but Micah knew what he was up to. What was his problem? Why wouldn't he let it go? He supposed it was just Emmett's personality. He didn't want to be left out if something was happening.

"Leave her alone, Emmett. You already know I'm trying not to get involved. You shouldn't, either. She has too much to be concerned about for romance right now. Especially with a SEAL." If he refused to give Emmett the reaction he wanted, maybe he would let it drop.

Besides, they needed to get down to business. "If I have it figured right, the target area is right under our noses. They must be disguising it somehow when they aren't working. They likely didn't expect any activity in the early-morning hours, which is why Keilani surprised them on her swim."

Emmett frowned, but he let his previous conversation topic go. "You think they know the routines?"

"Looks like it. That's not an easy feat, considering our crazy schedules." Micah drained the mug.

"They could have a spy." Emmett reached for the cup in Micah's hand and took both mugs to refill them.

When his phone buzzed, Micah picked it up as Emmett stepped into the kitchen, but before he could even read who the message was from, a scream pierced the silence. He rushed to the bathroom as his blood iced over.

FOUR

Micah dropped the phone into his pocket on his way to the bathroom door. "Keilani, are you okay? What's going on?"

The shower had shut off and now the bathroom was eerily silent. Finally, she answered him through the door, her voice small. "I'm fine. I'm sorry—I—I just panicked."

He thought for a beat before asking her what she meant. "What? Panicked over what?"

She spoke through the closed door again. "Just a minute. I'll show you."

He could hear her rustling around in the bathroom while he waited, reassuring him that she was physically unharmed. Finally, the door opened.

Her face was pale, even after being freshly scrubbed in the heat of the shower. "My phone chimed as I was turning off the water. When I checked the messages, I found that someone had sent me all of these pictures."

Keilani held out the burner phone Emmett had purchased for her before meeting with them. Micah needed to be sure he could stay in touch with her if she was out of his sight, but he'd only shared the number with his

CO, just in case something happened to him. How had someone already figured it out?

He took the phone from her trembling hand and began to scroll through photo after photo of Keilani, from her escape after her morning swim, to her introduction to the dolphins, and even her getting into Micah's truck. It was just short of being a photo documentary of everything she had done that day.

"These are images from the base's security cameras. Look at the time stamps." Micah scrolled through the images. "I think the guy wants us to know how close he is."

"Who has that kind of access? There's a picture of us in the dolphin enclosures. There is even one of us leaving the admiral's office." Keilani's voice was shaking. Her thoughts seemed pretty well aligned with his own. "And how did they get this number?"

She looked so small in Micah's clothes, his shorts rolled up at her tiny waist and the T-shirt hanging a bit lopsided off one shoulder. It only increased the vibes of vulnerability she was emitting. Micah steeled himself against the flood of protective emotions. Anger swelled within him, making him need to focus to keep it under control.

"It's definitely someone too close. There is no way a civilian could have accessed these photos. Even the best hacker in the world would have trouble pulling that off. A good zoom lens could explain some of them, but not all. And then there is the fact that the format is identical on every photo." The fear in her eyes heightened his protective instincts. "And the phone number… Well, they must have had someone following Emmett or got it somehow from the place he purchased it. Maybe he offered bribe money and the cashier took it."

Emmett stood out of the way, he noticed, taking in the scene. He wore a concerned look that said the gravity of Keilani's situation was finally sinking in. When Keilani didn't comment further, he stepped forward. "Is everything okay?"

Keilani nodded and crossed her arms over her midsection. "I'm sorry I worried everyone. I'm not normally so edgy."

"The perp has decided to stalk her on top of shooting at her and trying to blow her up." Micah held out the phone for Emmett to get a good look at the pictures. He scowled as he scrolled through them and then shook his head.

"Did anyone see you purchase the burner phone?" Micah knew Emmett would have been careful, but things just weren't making sense.

"No, the place was empty. I made sure of it." Emmett nodded his head for emphasis.

"Dude, that's messed up. How could it not be someone on the inside?" Emmett handed the phone back.

"I don't know, but we have to consider all of the possibilities." Micah motioned them both out of the hallway. As they entered the living room, Emmett offered Keilani a cup of coffee, but she shook her head.

"My stomach is a bit upset. I'd rather not eat or drink anything right now." She settled on the couch, but still looked terribly uncomfortable.

Emmett must have noticed. "I'll be outside taking care of some things in the yard if anyone needs me."

Micah nodded at him and watched him walk out the back door. "You're pretty safe here, you know."

Keilani made a visible effort to relax her form, but it wasn't completely effective. She only looked slightly less tense. "Thank you—for everything you've done today. This is not the kind of first impression I'd hoped to make." She was biting her lip again.

He watched her, hoping to think of a way to set her at ease. "No, probably not. But you aren't to blame."

His blunt response seemed to surprise her. Then she actually laughed and finally appeared to relax some.

"I already know a lot about you from your résumé," Micah said, determined to get her mind off all the worry, "so how about I tell you about me?"

"Okay. Where did you grow up?"

"I spent most of my young life on a farm in east Texas. But when I was fifteen, my dad died suddenly from pneumonia. My mom remarried and moved to Houston. It was completely different from small-town life. I had a huge adjustment period and went through some tough times before I settled in." That was an understatement, but he wasn't about to tell her what a wild kid he had once been. He was surprised at himself for telling her what he just had.

"Do you ever think about going back to farm life?" She smiled and he wondered what she was thinking about. Was she picturing him as an awkward, gangly teen? The thought made him uncomfortable and he wished he hadn't begun this discussion.

"Sometimes. I'll probably retire on a farm someday, depending on my health. There's a lot of hard work involved." He thought about how worn out his father had often seemed from farm life—dawn till dusk with no days off.

"My grandparents once worked on a pineapple plantation. They tell stories about the backbreaking work. They learned a great deal about life from the experience, though." Keilani touched a pattern on a sofa pillow she had pulled onto her lap.

"There's nothing like it." He watched her intently until her wide eyes met his again.

"Were you an only child?" She seemed almost as disconcerted as he felt in her presence. What was it about her that made him willing to open up in ways he usually avoided? He'd only had a glimpse of who she was deep down, but already there was an emotional connection to her that he couldn't explain. It wasn't just about her beauty, though she was lovely with her dark hair waving around her face. It was something he couldn't really explain.

"I have a half sister. After my mother remarried, she had Cadence, but with such a huge age gap, we've never been very close. My cousin from back in Sweetbriar is probably still more like a sibling to me. I keep in touch with Joel more than anyone." When he paused for a breath, Keilani nodded. The light from the living room window fell over her and she looked almost ethereal.

"What made you decide to become a navy SEAL?"

Now for the hard questions. Rather than answering right away, he deliberated over how much to tell her. How much would be enough? He had never told anyone everything.

"Well, I wound up in the navy because of some bad decisions. Let's just say my stepfather encouraged me to join the military. Once I realized that physical challenges proved to be a great way to channel my anger, one of my superiors suggested I consider SEAL training. I had my doubts at first, but eventually it worked out. Turned out it was a good fit for me."

If she wondered about his comment about dealing with his anger, she chose not to address it. He was grateful for that. Instead, she asked about the dolphins.

"How did you end up working with the mammals, then?"

"On one of our missions, we worked with the dolphin crews. The cetaceans accepted me well and one of the trainers at the time eventually recommended me to join the team. It just went forward from there."

Before Keilani could respond, Emmett came in the back door. "Micah, can I speak to you about something?"

Micah glanced at Keilani. "Stay put."

Emmett led him to the kitchen where he could see Keilani around the corner but they could talk without her hearing every word. "Micah, the security system has been compromised." He explained that where the fence separated their yard from the one behind them, the wires to the home security system rose up from a small pipe and along the fence for a short distance—and they'd all been severed. Keilani's whereabouts were certainly not a secret.

"I just happened to notice." Emmett put both hands on his hips.

"Someone has some breaking and entering plans on their agenda." Micah let out a frustrated breath. This guy didn't intend to cut them any slack.

"I'll get someone from the alarm company out here ASAP." Emmett already had his phone out to call.

Micah held out a hand to stop him. "Wait. If we know their plans, maybe we can be ready for them. It might be our best chance at catching our perp."

Emmett put his phone back in his pocket. "Okay, then. What's the plan?"

* * *

Keilani looked from one man to the other, wondering if this was how they always operated. They had come back into the living room wearing matching scowls. When they told her what had happened and began to explain their plans to try to catch the perpetrators in the act, she felt her stomach turn over. Of course, she knew SEALs were used to taking risks. But she was uncomfortable with the plan. She was going to be a little too close to someone who wanted her dead.

"So what if you're wrong? What if this person gets to me before you can stop him? I know he wants me dead." Her voice quavered just a bit.

"I'll see to it that doesn't happen." Micah's determined stance conveyed his confidence. It reassured Keilani somewhat.

"And you think this person will break in tonight?" She glanced around the room, wondering how her stalker would choose to break into the house. Would they know which room was hers and just come through her window? Or would they enter through the back door and secure the house first? She had no experience with how killers did things.

"I think it's likely. Honestly, I'm surprised it's been quiet for so long." Micah crossed his arms over his impossibly wide chest.

Don't think about how safe it would feel to be held there, Keilani chastised herself. But it was too late. She shook it off, reminding herself that trusting a man only led to pain and heartbreak. Her stepfather as well as her ex-boyfriend had taught her that.

"And Xavier and I will be here for backup." Emmett brought her attention back to the matter at hand, entirely too cheerful to be talking about someone trying to kill her.

Keilani smiled at Emmett, then noticed Micah looking between the two of them, frowning. Was he thinking she was being too friendly with Emmett? She only intended to show gratitude. Besides, why would he care? "That's reassuring."

Micah cleared his throat. "Okay, then, we are all clear on the plan?"

"Wait. So if I fall asleep and he breaks in my window, how will you know?" Keilani twisted her hands in her lap.

"You won't be sleeping in there. You'll stay in my room. It's more secure. I'll be in the hallway outside. Xavier will be on the couch and Emmett will be in your room. No matter what you hear, you'll stay put with the door locked until I text you the signal. Then you can come out if all is clear." Micah was wearing that frighteningly intense expression once more.

She swallowed hard. "You didn't tell me I would be staying in your room."

"Is there some reason that won't work?" His gray eyes scrutinized her face.

"No. I'm sure it will work just fine." Except that she would be occupying his most intimate personal space.

The sun was going down and the golden California streaks glistening over the horizon gilded the world outside the windows. It was peaceful and relaxed, a direct contrast to Keilani's tumultuous emotions. She suddenly felt very homesick for Hawaii and her family there. For once, she was second-guessing her personal choices.

Today's events had brought back too many disturbing memories. Being locked in the vault had felt suffocating, like all those times her stepfather had locked her in the closet when she was young. Her mind had conjured visions of the dark room with just a sliver of light, when the last thing she saw as he secured the door had always been that forbidding uniform.

She forced the memories away now. There was enough to worry about right now without letting the trauma of her past affect her mental state. She would focus on solving the problems of the day.

The hours passed slowly. Keilani met Xavier briefly before he went to shower. He was the quiet, studious type, if her first impression served her correctly.

Micah tried to distract her by telling her all about their dolphin program, but she was still painfully aware of the danger she was in. She caught herself peering out the window from time to time, watching for any unusual activity outside the house. She hadn't seen anything other than a few neighbors going about their business and the occasional child or pet outside playing on the sidewalks.

"Watching won't get this over with any faster. Do you like to read?" Micah's low voice close to her ear reminded her that they were now alone in the living room.

She turned slowly, careful not to bump into him since he was that close. She must have been half-asleep not to have noticed. He smelled warm and masculine and she almost forgot what he had asked.

"Yes, I do like to read. But I find it odd you didn't suggest TV or a movie instead." She cocked her head sideways and studied him.

"The remote is right beside you. I think if you really enjoyed watching TV you either would have asked or just turned it on by now." He was studying her in return, and she suddenly felt very self-conscious, wondering what he thought of her. Then she chastised herself for even caring.

"I like to watch television sometimes, but I enjoy reading more." She felt silly admitting it, maybe because he was still studying her face.

Emmett came in through the back door then, looking from one of them to the other, mischief on his face. "What's going on in here?"

"None of your business." Micah glared at him, but there was no bite to his tone.

"Cool. I brought dinner." His grin just broadened.

He held up two bags of takeout—In-N-Out burgers that smelled delicious. Keilani hadn't realized how hungry she was before now. Xavier joined them at the table as soon as he emerged from the shower, and they ate in near silence. Keilani noticed that the three men seemed to stay on full alert, even as they scarfed down their burgers and fries. She fought more than one yawn, fatigue settling in as the aftereffect of the adrenaline.

"You know, it probably wouldn't be a bad idea for you to get some rest while you can." Though he wasn't looking directly at her, Micah seemed to have noticed how hard she was fighting to stay awake. He was giving her an out.

"Yeah, I'm a little tired." Keilani picked up her trash and began to clean up after the guys. The action was met with immediate protests, Emmett insisting on handling the small bit of cleanup.

"Come on. I'll show you where everything is." Micah stood and held out a hand. She almost took it until she realized that wasn't what he intended. He was just motioning her forward. He dropped it as she started in his direction.

His room wasn't what she would have expected. It was neat and perfect, of course, but she had somehow thought it would be more sparsely furnished. Instead, it had a warm, homey feeling to it. A deep blue coverlet accented by a bold cardinal splash of pillows and a cream throw stretched atop his queen-size bed. Pine furniture and braided rugs topped off the masculine design, and pictures of family and military friends graced the dresser. A couple of candles gave off a faint scent that reminded her of Micah, and the walls were fitted with shelves organizing everything from a flag representing a deceased military loved one to awards Micah had apparently won at various times during his career. A wingback chair in cream-and-navy-striped fabric sat by the curtained window.

The most surprising thing, however, was the trunk in one corner. It looked like an antique—brass fasteners and leather straps telling the story of its functionality while scuff marks indicated it had once been used well. The top of it held a frame filled to the corners with pictures of Micah and what must be his grandmother at various stages in his life. A stuffed tiger sat on one edge and a lace handkerchief on the opposite side. There was a framed letter as well, clearly in a woman's handwriting, which Keilani could only assume was from his grandmother. The edges of it were frayed as if he had carried it with him and read it many times.

"My paternal grandmother died right after I began SEAL training. She never told me she was sick." He spoke behind her in a slightly hoarse voice. "I don't know how long she knew she had cancer."

Keilani's heart sank. "You weren't there when she died."

She turned in time to see him shake his head. "That's the last letter she ever wrote me. She never once even hinted that she wasn't well."

"You two were close before you left?" Keilani knew the answer from the evidence, but she wanted to hear the details.

"She was my only remaining link to my father. He passed ten years ago in a plane crash. Even after my dad died, Mom would let me go stay with my grandmother for a few weeks every summer. Before Dad was killed, sometimes he was able to take vacations and we would all go for a few weeks. Those were the best days of my young life." Micah's smile faded as if he felt he had said too much.

He straightened. "There are extra blankets in the closet outside the door if you get cold. I'll just grab the things I need for the night and get out of your way."

Keilani watched him without speaking for a moment. She wanted him to continue talking about his life, but it was apparent he didn't feel comfortable doing so. "Thank you. Again, I'm sorry for the circumstances."

Micah gathered a handful of his things and moved toward the door.

Keilani watched him go and tried to decide whether to just settle into the bed or sit in the chair for a little while and think. The chair won out, considering she needed some time to calm her mind. She pulled the throw from Micah's bed and settled it around her, inhaling his scent.

No matter what her first impression of Micah might have been, she was beginning to see the kindness of his heart. She hadn't wanted to like him—at least, not past the tolerance necessary between coworkers. And then there was the situation with the World Animal Protection Agency and Gretchen's request to report back, which made her feel guilty. She didn't want to tell him they suspected he was taking inadequate care of his cetaceans. He seemed to know they were under some suspicion, but rumors were different than actually being accused.

But despite what she wanted in any of these areas, she found she was softening toward him, more all the time, actually. It frightened her. For the most part, men had never been anything but trouble in her life. Her stepfather had always viewed her as a bit of a nuisance. And that didn't even begin to describe her stepbrother. He was a monster. Her grandfather had been the only exception.

She could relate to Micah's loss, although her father was still very much alive. He simply chose to have nothing to do with her. He might as well no longer exist. Unfortunately, her experience with dating hadn't been much better.

A quick knock announced Micah's return. "Sorry. Forgot something."

"It's okay." Keilani rose as he entered. He moved to the nightstand to retrieve something from the drawer before turning back to look at her.

"What's wrong? Is the bed too hard?" Micah glanced at the offending furniture even as she shook her head.

"No, the bed is fine. I mean… I just haven't been able to settle down yet." She felt awkward standing in his bedroom while he scrutinized her. She clasped her hands and unclasped them, bit her lip and then ran both hands down the front of her thighs.

"Okay. Well, if you need anything just ask." He started to go, then paused again. "And, Keilani?"

"Hm?" She tried not to watch his mouth, but her eyes seemed to have their own will.

"I don't blame any of this on you. You should know that the navy was investigating the area drug trafficking routes before you came. You just happened to be in the wrong place at the wrong time." He watched her and she felt heat creep into her cheeks. Did he realize what she was thinking? She was getting a little too attached to the idea of having him around to protect her.

The moment was shattered by the sound of breaking glass. Keilani gasped and Micah was instantly on the offensive. His entire demeanor changed in a flash.

"Pretty bold move to make so much noise. Must be trying to create a distraction." Keilani realized he was speaking his thoughts aloud for her benefit. He moved to stand before her like a shield. "Stay with me."

"Location?" Xavier called from the far end of the house.

Both Micah and Emmett called out answers in a number code. Xavier returned with his also. Then he spouted off something else she didn't understand. When she looked questioningly at Micah he leaned in close and whispered to her, "The intruder tried to come in through the bathroom window. At least, that's what he wants us to think." He urged her down behind the bed, away from the window.

Emmett called out something else she didn't catch. "What?" She kept her voice to a whisper.

"Emmett called the police. They will be here in five."

He looked a bit perturbed not to be in the middle of the action, but he answered her patiently enough.

A hail of bullets began to rain down on the house. Another window shattered, this one just across the hall, and from the sounds coming from the back door, she could only assume the men had broken in there.

"I guess they didn't like it that we didn't fall for their little distraction." Micah had his Sig in his hand, and he winked at her before leaning around the door to see where the men were.

A string of ugly remarks from the man who had entered the back door filled the air in the hall, but the second intruder had now discovered their hiding place. He burst through the door and dove for Keilani, but she rolled out of his reach.

The first man returned then.

"Micah!" She knew he was already on it, but she wanted him to hurry. He had turned toward the man, ready to fire, but before he could the masked man yanked at Keilani again, this time managing to pull her over in front of him like a shield. Micah jerked the nose of his gun up at the last second, leaving Keilani to wince at the near miss. She squeezed her eyes shut.

"Let her go." His voice was a frightening roar. "You're surrounded and outnumbered."

Keilani looked around to see that what Micah said was true. The other man was now hog-tied on the rug and Xavier and Emmett stood on either side of Keilani and her captor, Micah right in front of them.

The man in the mask just laughed. "But you're out-maneuvered."

He jabbed a cold-nosed gun into Keilani's temple and she jerked, but he only tightened his grip on her.

She could feel the pounding of her pulse in every part of her body. All of her senses seemed heightened, the man's strange smell too strong in her nose, the sound of his breathing loud and overwhelming. But worst of all was the rough grip he held on her arm, twisting and threatening her wordlessly while the hateful stab of metal prodded her temple.

Time seemed to have switched to slow motion, Micah staring at the gun aimed at her, and then assessing her captor carefully. What was he thinking? Did he consider, even for a second, just letting him take her away? Getting out of this mess seemed impossible.

But then Micah looked at her face, his eyes narrowed slightly, and to her shock a small grin pulled at one corner of his mouth. "That's what you think."

Keilani couldn't see her captor, but she could imagine his smug grin slipping from place as he considered Micah's comment.

Everything happened at once.

It was so confusing to Keilani that she really didn't even know how it all happened. She just relied on Micah to see her through. Her feet were knocked out from under her a split second before something flew at the masked man, his gun firing as Micah's muscular frame covered Keilani's own on the floor. She wasn't sure where any of the yelling came from. Breathing was her sole concern as she lay on the floor praying God would keep them all safe.

Sirens wailed into the driveway about the time Emmett declared the invaders to all be secured. Micah helped her up, looking her over for any injuries. He gave a satisfied nod and then went to talk to the officer asking Xavier questions.

It was ridiculous that she was so offended by his actions, but would it have hurt him to actually ask if she was okay? The men didn't even spare her another glance as they went over the events of the evening. They were talking quickly and almost like excited boys about the past few minutes. It felt like she wasn't even in the room.

At least her seeming invisibility had one bonus—they weren't worried about shielding her from the truth. And now she knew that during all the chaos, the man who had held her at gunpoint had somehow managed to free himself and slip out a window while they were securing the other man in the back of the police car. It seemed impossible, but just like that, he was gone, leaving the ropes that Xavier had carefully secured him with behind in an unassuming heap on the floor.

She shivered as she thought about the feel of his steel grip on her arm and the cold contact of the gun against her skin. Her eyes filled before she could blink the tears away. What would have happened if Micah hadn't been there?

Keilani straightened her T-shirt and took herself to bed. If the authorities wanted to question her, they would have to come looking for her.

The attack had been too real, too much of a close call. She was unsettled by it.

It seemed that at least one of the men who wanted her dead was more than prepared to deal with a houseful of SEALs.

FIVE

Micah watched Keilani stomp off to bed and wondered what had upset her. Maybe she thought the man had come close to capturing her. She didn't seem to have a clue that the weak plan those men had concocted didn't even stand a chance. He reminded himself that most people really had no idea what SEALs were capable of.

He refocused his attention on the task at hand, deciding to let Keilani rest for the moment. There would be time to make sure she was okay once the heavy stuff was done.

He entered her room almost an hour later after a quick knock. When he spoke her name, she sat up in the bed. He expected her to be groggy, but instead she just looked angry.

"Hey, are you okay? I knocked you to the ground pretty hard." He almost sat on the edge of her bed, and then thought better of it and moved to the chair near the end instead.

"I'm fine." Her voice was flat. He frowned in the dark.

"Are you sure? You don't really sound like it."

"Why all the concern now? I'm great, okay? It's been

a very long day. I just want to sleep." She began a little loudly, then seemed to calm herself.

He let out a breath and then stood. "Okay. You're right, it's been rough. Get a good night's sleep. We'll head back to the base at 0600."

"Leave at six?" Her voice squeaked.

"I thought I'd let you sleep a little later, considering the day you've had." He gave her a tight smile and grabbed the doorknob to close it behind him.

She grunted as he closed the door, and he headed to his makeshift bed in the living room. His schedule varied based on the training required of SEALs, but he would try to keep to a regular schedule while working with Keilani. He could explain the rest later. There would no doubt be times he couldn't keep to the same hours.

The fact that she still seemed upset had him a little concerned, but maybe she just had too much on her mind to settle in and sleep just yet.

He spent so much time with his brothers on the SEAL team that he forgot how to act around females sometimes. He thought of his little sister and what it would be like if she were in Keilani's place. Cadence was only eight now, but the idea of her being in danger freaked him out, even though they didn't spend much time together.

The truth was, he was just as worried about Keilani being in danger. She was getting under his skin somehow, though he hadn't known her long. Her soft and sweet smile, the tender care she had shown when he introduced her to the dolphins, her grace and kindness, even in the face of danger, all added up to someone he would love to spend more time with.

If he didn't have goals... And phobias.

His future plans had never included a wife and family. It was one of the things that made him such a great warrior—he didn't have any of those familial ties causing him anxiety over how they might handle it if he were killed. He never wanted to lose that edge, especially not for something as volatile as family. A family could be lost at any time. Like his dad. And the idea that he might never be enough...well, that didn't help matters, either.

"Micah, you okay?" Xavier stuck his head around the doorway.

"Yeah. Fine. What's up?" He suddenly realized Xavier had already spoken to him once.

"Just letting you know the window is patched up for the time being and security specialists will be out to fix the alarm first thing in the morning." He paused. "I'll be up. Get some rest."

Micah knew Xavier was trying to help, but he also knew he probably wouldn't really be able to sleep. "I'd like to, but..."

Xavier nodded. "I understand. But be a SEAL. Shut it off. Do what you gotta do."

Xavier was right. He needed to exercise some control over the situation. It was all mental. It was *always* mental. The heart and emotions had nothing to do with it.

At six o'clock the next morning, Keilani was ready and drinking coffee at the kitchen table when Micah left his bedroom.

"This is terrible. Remind me to get some good Kona coffee before tomorrow morning." She grimaced at her cup.

He chuckled. "Yes, ma'am." Then he poured himself a cup of the *terrible* coffee.

She was probably hoping that any discussion about last night could wait until later in the day, if he were to judge from her expression. He was in no mood to oblige her, however. He sat down across from her, knowing full well that they needed to get going. "I spoke to the detective this morning. The guy we caught was just a hired thug. According to the investigators, he wouldn't give up the ringleader."

She closed her eyes for a moment before looking up at him with a nod. "I had decided he must be."

Now he was intrigued. "Oh? And why is that?"

She shrugged. "There are a few reasons."

"Starting with?" He really wanted to know now.

She clasped both hands around the cup. "First of all, the intruders last night were too small to be any of the men I saw yesterday morning. Also, those guys didn't have the stamina of the man who chased me to the beach. The attacker was breathing hard just trying to catch me, and he seemed to be in charge of the group that attacked last night. The men I saw swimming were tall, fit and more commanding in presence, even underwater."

He raised an eyebrow. "You noticed all that?"

She lifted one shoulder. "Yes, when I really thought about it. But to begin with, it was just a feeling I had."

"I've had to learn to trust my instincts. It wasn't easy. You're blessed that it comes so naturally to you." He took a long sip. This coffee really wasn't all that bad.

"Trusting your instincts is important when working with animals. Speaking of which, shouldn't we be going?" She met his eyes then.

"Yes. Let's get to it." He stood and downed the coffee. "We'll also get you more clothes this afternoon."

Xavier had brought in a couple of things for her the night before so she would have something to wear this morning. There were a few female naval officers that lived close by and Xavier had been trying to get a date with one of them. It provided a good excuse for him to visit her.

"Okay. I'd like to meet Sarah and tell her thank you for loaning me the clothes." Keilani followed him out.

"I'm sure Xavier would be more than willing to return them for you." He couldn't suppress the chuckle. She giggled, too, and his heart gave a little thud. Not good.

The base was pretty quiet and the admiral had posted extra guards around the dolphin enclosures just as he had promised. They checked Micah's ID thoroughly and frowned when Keilani presented the shiny new one the navy had given her the day before. It was obvious that Micah struggled to keep his impatience in check as the man did his job. One thing was certain—he was ready to get to work.

Keilani picked up on his methods quickly and shared several tips of her own. He found their interactions and experiences with the dolphins were pretty similar, other than the military aspect of his own, and she had some great ideas for improving the safety and contentedness of the animals.

By the time they finished up hours later, he was even more impressed with Keilani than before. Not only did the dolphins take to her with an ease he had never seen before, but she also managed them with a stern but gentle hand. They responded beautifully.

Under Suspicion

Once they finished, he congratulated her on a job well-done. "You have about a thirty-minute break to relax, or whatever you want to do. Then shower and get dressed and I'll show you to the mess hall for lunch."

She asked if she could use the indoor pool to get some cardio in for the day, and he pointed to where she should go. When she disappeared in the direction of the fitness facilities, he headed off to the men's showers to try to clear his own mind before attending to his paperwork. He had too many thoughts of Keilani to shake off right now. This might turn out to be even harder than he thought.

Keilani sighed as she slid into the warm water of the indoor pool. The base had amazing workout facilities and she had been eyeing this pool area since she arrived. She loved swimming, and getting some laps in was just what she needed to refocus.

A whole five hours of work this morning with no danger. Maybe it was because of the extensive network of guards surrounding them. Maybe her instincts had been wrong this time. She had expected another attack before now.

She moved slowly, floating atop the water, and closed her eyes, replaying the hours spent with the dolphins. It was obvious that Micah cared deeply for the animals, so any ideas that he might be involved in the rumored mistreatment were simply out of the question. In fact, it seemed impossible to her that there could be any mistreatment of the animals at all with him overseeing the program. The people from the World Animal Protection Agency would be receiving her report as soon as she could compose one.

This afternoon Micah planned to go over the problems needing to be addressed in the new program with her more extensively, focusing on the prevention of drug smuggling in the area. It wouldn't be much different from the bomb detection the dolphins were accustomed to, but the new substance might present a challenge she hadn't anticipated. The navy wanted to get the pressing problem under control before the news got out to the public. It was basically a local war against a drug cartel that was using any means possible to get their goods into the country. However they were smuggling the drugs through undetected was making the navy look foolish, according to Micah. And it was up to the dolphin team to put a stop to it.

But none of that would explain the rumors of sick and suffering cetaceans, and even suggestions that many may be dying. She wanted to know what was going on.

Something felt off, and not just with the dolphins.

The water was soothing and comforting at first, but after a few moments in the enclosed area, she began to feel a bit disoriented. Dismissing it as the aftereffects of shock, she just kept swimming and tried to push through it. Dizziness continued to wash over her in waves, however. She paused at the end of the pool nearest the door when she realized her arms were starting to feel weak and uncoordinated. The enclosed space surrounding the pool began to spin, slowing down as she tried to reach for the ladder. She stopped grasping for a moment, then realized her brain and her surroundings were not moving in sync any longer. Nausea hit her like the breaking surf and her heart jerked out of rhythm and began to race. She blinked, trying to think.

Slowly, the realization came to her. Someone was gassing the indoor pool.

Using her last bit of strength to yank her form out of the water, she grabbed a towel as quickly as she could manage and clumsily wrapped it around her. She stumbled toward the door and managed to get it open, gulping in a breath of clean air just before everything began to go black.

"Micah!" she called, but she knew it was a weak cry, likely too faint to be heard. She tried to walk out, but her knees refused to keep her upright any longer as her muscles gave way to the effects of the gas. She pitched forward, then crawled a few steps, dragging herself with what little strength she had left in her forearms, all the while struggling to hold on to her towel. In a matter of seconds, the world went completely black.

Micah's deep voice was the next thing Keilani remembered. "Keilani, can you hear me?"

He was kneeling beside her, but she wasn't on the floor outside the exercise pool any longer. She heard beeping and there was a tube running out from under a sheet covering the top of her. An occasional humming from the blood pressure monitor registered in her foggy thoughts and she could smell the vague antiseptic odor of hospital around her. A plaque on the wall bearing a military seal confirmed it was the naval hospital, and waning light from the window meant she had passed much of the afternoon here in this bed.

"I—hear you." Keilani tried to sit up, but a fierce pain in her head prevented it.

"I was beginning to wonder if you would wake."

Micah leaned over her. "Do you remember what happened?"

"I was in the pool and I just started to feel weak and dizzy. Someone must have been pumping gas into the pool room—someone who knew I was in there." Keilani spoke slowly, trying not to make it too difficult on her head.

"I thought I heard you call, but by the time I got there, you were out cold. I wasn't sure why, so the doctors had to determine how to treat you. It's taken us all afternoon to figure it out." Micah's hair was mussed, giving testament to his agitation, and Keilani found it unexpectedly endearing.

"I'm surprised you heard me. I could barely hold my head up at the time." Keilani pulled her arm from beneath the blanket and studied the IV.

"It's fortunate I did. The doctors tell me that a few more minutes of exposure to the gas could have killed you. That was smart thinking getting out of there when you did." Micah ran a vein-studded hand through his hair now. "I can't even leave you alone for ten minutes."

"I'm so sorry. I've been nothing but trouble since my arrival. I think it's time we go check out the reef where I saw those men. Maybe it will give us a clue about how to put an end to all this." Keilani winced, not just because her head throbbed, but also because things weren't exactly going well at her new job.

"You aren't taking that chance. You're already in enough danger. I'll take a boat out with Xavier and Emmett tonight." He frowned.

"And leave me alone? I'd rather you didn't. And how will you know where to look without taking me along?"

She watched his face, knowing he couldn't argue with that logic.

He hesitated for a long time and she could only imagine what thoughts were battling in his head. "Fine. But only if the doctor okays it."

Keilani nodded. "Good. I have a few ideas about how I might be able to lure the men back to the area so you guys could catch them."

"What? I don't think so. We're just going to look around." Micah gripped the chair with both hands. "You'll stay on the boat."

"We'll see." But she had no intention of doing so.

SIX

Though Keilani was declared fit and released, Micah wasn't about to let her go back to the base. The admiral okayed the remainder of the afternoon off so Keilani could recover and Micah could keep watch for any other problems. He made her promise to rest in preparation to go look for the drop site that evening.

Micah tucked her into some blankets on the sofa before calling to speak to his friend Paul on the investigation team.

"Looks like a botched attempt at cyanide gas. The culprit must not have realized that pool deck isn't airtight enough to cause asphyxiation with such small amounts of the gas. If the room had been better sealed, she would have died before you found her." Paul explained that he had reached this conclusion after examining a blood sample from the hospital.

"That's not too reassuring. How am I going to keep her alive, Paul?" Micah gripped the phone against his ear.

"You have to be very diligent. The guy seems desperate. And this is four attempts in two days." Paul's voice rang with concern.

"At this rate there will be at least two more before the night is over." Micah heard the fatigue in his own voice. "I can't let her out of my sight until this is over."

"Definitely not." Paul paused. "There is one thing I wanted to ask you about."

Micah waited, saying simply, "What's that?"

"It seems like Dr. Lucas happening upon the drug operation might have been a trigger. But if she saw it where you are telling me she did, it's very close to the dolphin enclosures. It might not just be because of what she saw that she is being targeted. Have you considered these smugglers might be using your dolphins?"

Micah drew in a quick breath. "I have reason to believe they might be using dolphins in their smuggling, but not mine—not the navy's dolphins."

"And who's looking after them now?" Paul's voice held a slight edge.

"That's a good question. Admiral McLeary said no one was to go near them besides Keilani and me. They are under constant guard. I don't really know anymore if that means anything, though."

"Does he suspect the dolphins are at risk?" Paul's voice rose a little.

Micah felt a little bad about not considering that before. "Maybe so. I guess I should have asked that question myself. At the time, I just assumed it was to keep Keilani safer while we worked."

"I'd find out what is going on with them in your absence if I were you." Paul clicked his tongue. "In fact, I think I'll check into that myself."

Micah hung up, feeling out of sorts.

He put off telling Keilani the news, mostly because not talking to her much was the closest he could get to avoiding her at the moment. His tumultuous emotions needed a break and his assignment—not to mention her safety—meant he must keep her close. And all that led to more of that protective instinct and more tender feelings, so he just needed to distance himself emotionally.

Keilani didn't seem to notice. She had a notebook and his laptop on the sofa beside her. Every so often she would stop scrolling and write something down. His curiosity finally got to him and he had to ask.

"What are you working on?"

She jumped, confirming she had completely forgotten he was in the room. "Oh. Uh, there are some vague news reports on dolphins being used to help underwater drug smugglers. Nothing by big news publications, but still worth looking into. I was gathering all the information on it that I could, just in case that's what we have here."

He squirmed a little. Why hadn't he thought of doing that? She had completely blown his focus. "And when were you going to let me in on this?"

She paused to write something else down. "I was going to give you a summary of what I found later. You seemed a little preoccupied just now. Like you didn't want to talk."

As Keilani went back to scrolling, Micah studied her. How did she do that so easily? "You don't think there's any chance someone is using navy dolphins, I hope."

She shrugged. "You don't think someone on the inside could be helping drug smugglers and trying to kill me."

"I said I wasn't sure."

"Neither am I."

"Is there any other way someone could have taken those photos?" She glanced hopefully at him.

"I can't think of any."

Their eyes met. An enemy outside was one thing, but an enemy within was a terrifying thought. And getting more terrifying all the time.

Micah moved to sit beside her on the sofa, but then he instantly regretted it. The heat that passed between them when their arms brushed made him forget about everything but her nearness. He sucked in a long breath and realized she had stopped scrolling and sat perfectly still.

"What are you doing?" Her voice was soft and low.

"I just wanted to see what you're finding." He pretended to focus on the screen until her eyes met his own.

"I said I would tell you what I found." She seemed edgy, nervous.

"I'd just prefer to jump in along the way. Don't worry, I'll catch up quickly." He'd better, or his thoughts were going to take off in directions he didn't want or need them to.

She handed him her notes, then turned the laptop at an angle to help him see it better. He didn't move away like she probably hoped he would, although he knew he should have. He wanted to breathe in her sweet scent a little longer. Despite her current danger, she made him feel a sense of peace he hadn't experienced in longer than he cared to remember.

"Micah—" She started to speak, but then shook her head as if trying to take back the single spoken word.

He didn't want to respond and discourage her from speaking whatever was on her mind, so he just waited.

She never got a chance to complete the thought, however. Shattering glass alerted them to another attack, and before Keilani could dump the computer onto the sofa beside her, Micah scooped her into his arms and ran. She was obviously confused as to what was happening, but he didn't take time to explain. She would understand soon enough.

They dove out the back door just as the blast shook the living room. Keilani shrieked and he looked over his shoulder to see the curtains go up in flames.

"What was that?" Keilani was shaking violently now.

"Molotov cocktail. A pretty good one, too. They aren't messing around. Let's go." He set her on her feet but tugged her away from the house.

When the shots began, he gestured toward her. "Stay low. They are going to keep shooting."

Her brow furrowed. "But they just tried to blow us up."

"That's not what a Molotov cocktail is for. It's mostly just to drive you out so you are an easier target." He gave her another tug.

"Oh, to shoot at me. Fantastic. 'Cause I haven't been shot at in a couple of hours." Keilani shook her head. "I'm sorry I'm so inexperienced at running for my life."

"Actually, you're getting way more experience than I'd like you to have." Micah urged her on. They ducked through the gate and fled across a neighbor's yard. "Good thing most of my neighbors are navy. They won't be too surprised that the SEALs are getting shot at again." He winked at her, trying to lighten the mood.

"I guess it's just an everyday job hazard for you?" Keilani's voice was only a little sarcastic.

"Not quite every day. Just with you around." He grinned at her audaciously before taking her hand and pulling her behind a neighboring house.

A bullet ricocheted off the brick by their heads and he started tugging her along again. "Oops, time to move."

He was purposely trying to keep things light. He didn't know how much more she could deal with before melting down, and he needed to keep her functional until they lost their pursuer.

He saw a black SUV round the corner by a house diagonal from them, and a flash of familiar light against the tinted window told him a gun was inside.

"Get down! There's our shooter."

Keilani obeyed, looking bewildered as more shots pinged around them sporadically. Their guy had lost sight of them. Now maybe he would give up.

It wasn't as easy as he'd hoped, however. Knowing they couldn't have escaped that quickly without being seen, the men in the SUV made a couple more loops around the block, prompting Micah to push Keilani back and forth around corners and behind storage sheds to keep them hidden from view.

The SUV slowed, the Glock glinting in the interior lights. "They see us. Run for it." Micah gave her a slight push, intending to stay at her back.

Just as they took off across another lawn, however, the sirens became audible in the distance and the squeal of tires accompanied them as the SUV sped away. A few random bullets peppered the air as if the shooter hoped to get in a cheap shot on the way out.

"Keilani." He tugged her to a stop. "They're gone."

She practically fell into his arms in relief. From her expression, he feared she would break into tears at any moment.

"Are you okay? You weren't hit anywhere, were

you?" He ran his hands gently up and down her arms and she shivered in response.

"I'm fine. I'm—I'm not fine. How long? How long will this continue?" She was shaking all over. He had to fight the urge to take her into his arms and comfort her. But he knew holding her close wouldn't do either of them any favors.

Keilani stumbled forward, though, and left him no choice.

She knew she shouldn't let him hold her like this, but right now Keilani needed comfort, no matter how fleeting. She kept telling herself not to get attached to him because he wouldn't be around for long, but her heart seemed to have its own ideas, and those ideas definitely included softening toward Micah Kent.

If it wasn't for the dolphins—her first love—she would probably be headed back across the Pacific by now. She missed Grandma Loni and her best friend Jacquie. It probably wouldn't be hard to get her old job back at the aquatic park where she'd worked as a marine veterinarian before coming to California.

She had received a message that morning from her friend Gretchen with the World Animal Protection Agency and had hoped to find more evidence to prove that any abuse of the local dolphins wasn't Micah's fault before reporting back to her. She had simply replied that so far everything seemed to be just fine.

She had been searching out articles that might tell her what to look for, though, and investigating who might be reporting such slander against the navy, when Micah had gotten involved. She had quickly modified her search, but she needed to tell him soon.

She shivered as her mind returned to the recent events. She tried not to dwell on how much she was beginning to rely on Micah, and particularly how much she enjoyed being able to draw comfort from him. She would be better off back on the island. Safer, both physically and emotionally. After her past experiences with men, she didn't want to risk her heart when she knew how much pain it could cause. The last time she had believed in love, her heart had been completely crushed when she discovered it was entirely one-sided. She had no desire to feel that kind of heartbreak again.

"We're going to end this." Micah was trying to reassure her, even as her thoughts were fleeing back to Hawaii. "But first, maybe we need to get your mind off things. How about a swim?"

She pulled away from him for a second. "With the dolphins?"

He nodded. "Just for fun. No training, no pressure."

"That sounds great." She relaxed against him, but instantly regretted it. She bolted upright. He was watching her when she turned, but his guarded expression told her little of what he was thinking.

Keilani breathed in the calm of her favorite environment. The dolphin pools were quiet, and as she slid into the comfort of the crystal-blue waters, Micah pulled a few switches to allow some of the dolphins to swim in. Keilani floated quietly, waiting for the animals to remember her.

The females swam up to her right away, especially Nikita, who seemed to remember her well. Mulan was more interested in asserting her authority, butting Nikita with her nose and angling her flippers just right to splash Keilani. The males finally swam over, Rambo rubbing against her in search of affection. Stefan hung back, clearly curious.

"Mind if I introduce a couple more of the team members to the mix? Carbon and Mitzie are young, but they like to play. It would do them good to socialize with the more mature crowd." Micah gestured in the direction of a glassed gate where two smaller dolphins observed them with interest.

"Oh, sure. The more, the merrier." Keilani laughed and waved to the youngsters, who zipped in as Micah opened the glass gate.

Like puppies, the two young dolphins swam crazily around her in search of attention. She responded by remaining still as they bounced some squeaks of various pitches off her and then began clicking rhythmically as they checked her out. Keilani laughed, causing Carbon, the darkest in color of the half-dozen dolphins, to dart away, sluicing through the water in surprise.

"I'm sorry, little one. You're just so cute." Keilani moved softly, encouraging him back to her.

Micah joined them in the water then. "Come on, kids. Let's show Keilani what you can do."

At Micah's command, the veteran dolphins began to put on a show. Not only could they sniff out enemy bombs and identify foreign swimmers, but Micah's dolphins could rescue the drowning, flip switches, tumble small boats as a team, and put on a regular Sea World show of flips, dives and driving humans through the water using their strong noses. Keilani clapped and laughed, and even the young dolphins wanted in on the performance. Micah showed Keilani how to give the navy commands and she worked with the veterans as well as the babies. Micah commented positively on her aptitude for both learning and teaching. For a little while Keilani almost forgot about being hunted like a wild creature, shot at and threatened. She just enjoyed the freedom and the feel of the water, the joyful squeals and clicks of the dolphins and the playful abandon on Micah's face.

That was the most startling, and far more dangerous to her heart. The tough, steely navy SEAL was transformed before her eyes, to more of a playful boy, at one with the mammals he loved so much. His gray eyes crinkled with a laughing smile, glowing with a joy she felt on a deeper level, down in her soul. Perfect white teeth under his full lips, visible where his head bobbed just above the water, were flashing back at her every time she laughed.

She had never known anyone else to enjoy the dolphins this much besides herself. It was like a mirror of her own reactions to the animals. All her reservations fled.

No, she couldn't be letting emotion get to her. She couldn't be so easily taken in by a man. Thoughts rushed to her mind of another man she had once believed had tender qualities. It had been a scam. She couldn't believe it so easily again.

Keilani pushed those memories to the back of her mind. She couldn't think about them now, couldn't think about Micah as anything but her coworker. She couldn't like him. Not even a little. Right now she would just bask in the feeling of not looking over her shoulder, heart pounding in fear. This moment would be over too soon anyway.

"Let's give them their rewards and feed everyone.

They're going to be worn out. We also need to doctor Schwartz. He got a little too enthusiastic playing with one of the older males and the other dolphin got aggressive. He has some cuts that need to be treated."

Micah swam over and helped her from the pool before leading her to the supplies they would need for doctoring the wounded dolphin. She examined the wound to make sure the cuts were healing properly and recommended an ointment that might be effective at speeding up the healing process. She knew it was common for male dolphins to play aggressively and even fight, but she hated seeing the teeth scrapes on the young dolphin's skin. Though it was part of the natural order of things, she wished it didn't happen.

After they fed all the dolphins, Micah also asked her to look at another one who needed attention.

"She's not necessarily unhealthy. There's just something about Rhianna that seems off somehow." Micah led her to the dolphin in question as he explained. "It might be nothing, but it's a feeling I have. Maybe her change in attitude shouldn't be ignored and all."

Keilani murmured her agreement and began a thorough examination of the dolphin. Rhianna didn't want to cooperate at first, but as Keilani spoke softly to her and persisted with her gentle palpations, she eventually relented.

Not long into her exam, Keilani noticed a hard place on the dolphin's abdomen. It was just enough to make her curious, but closer investigation caused her some alarm. Maybe it was nothing, but it seemed to need more exploration.

She looked up at Micah with lips pressed tightly together.

"What is it?" He wore a look of grave concern.

"I'm not positive, but it feels like a tracking chip. I'm afraid I'm going to have to examine her more closely to be sure." She gave Rhianna a reassuring rub.

"You mean exploratory surgery?" Micah's concern was evident.

"Maybe nothing that drastic, but she probably needs a sedative, and we'll need to put her in a secure holding pen." She winced. "Hopefully, I'm wrong."

"If you're not…" He trailed off, but she knew what he was thinking. It would be his worst nightmare.

And it certainly wouldn't take the drug runners long to realize she wasn't in her usual holding area if they were tracking her.

It was heartbreaking to think someone would use an innocent animal for such a terrible purpose. "It also doesn't really explain her attitude change."

He ran a hand through his still-damp hair. "You think there's more?"

She nodded. "Most likely."

Micah rubbed Rhianna's head. "I should have kept a closer eye on you, girl."

"She'll be okay. But we need to take care of this as quickly as possible."

While Micah prepared a holding pen and got Rhianna prepped for the procedure, Keilani called her mentor, a marine vet named Dr. Carmen Segall.

"How do I identify and treat a cetacean who has been exposed to unknown illegal substances?" Keilani asked quietly. "This wasn't really covered thoroughly in vet school."

Dr. Segall made an agreeing noise. "No, and I hoped you'd never have to deal with such an event. But working with navy dolphins, I suppose it's a different arena. Fortunately, though, I've had some experience there, just not much. What symptoms present?"

"Just a change in attitude and appetite. There's a hard place on her abdomen, but it's small and I suspect it's a tracking device the drug runners are using to keep up with her." Keilani kept her voice low, peering over her shoulder. She knew Micah probably already suspected what was happening, but she didn't want to alarm him unnecessarily if Rhianna wasn't being used as a drug mule.

"Hmm. Probably, but it could be something else. Most of the time the easiest place to insert a device like you're describing is in the upper anterior portion. If you can check that out without having to use invasive procedures, that should give you a clue," Dr. Segall explained. "I'd recommend ultrasound."

"Of course. I'll check it out. Hopefully, I'm wrong."

"Keilani, have you reported this to anyone?" Dr. Segall's voice was low and soft.

"Of course not. I just discovered it." She explained how it had occurred.

"Right. Well, I don't need to remind you that the welfare of the animals comes first."

Fresh guilt swept over her. What would be the ethical thing to do? She hadn't mentioned the suspicions that Gretchen wanted her to check on to Micah. She wanted to protect him, but she didn't know why. She hadn't had time to process everything and it was making her head spin.

"Yes, I know. I have a duty to protect them. But I can't report anything until I have facts. And there is also the protocol of the US Navy to consider. I need to know what exactly is going on before I speak to anyone. The navy is doing the best they can with these dolphins. I just have to figure out what could have been done to prevent this, if anything."

"Just be sure that you do. I know you have always had strong ethics. Don't let the navy intimidate you." Dr. Segall spoke gently, but her words resonated.

After a few more minutes of discussion in which Dr. Segall advised her on care and treatment, Keilani disconnected and went to join Micah and Rhianna. "I think we'd best do an ultrasound before we do anything else."

He turned to study her at the announcement. "Of course. I guess I should have thought of that. I'll have to gather up the equipment we need and the mobile sonogram unit."

When they had everything together, they positioned Rhianna with a sling designed to hold her most of the way out of the water, rubbed her down gently with diaper rash ointment to keep her skin moistened and sedated her. Keilani looked at Micah as they waited, letting the dolphin settle. She let out a few cries in protest of her capture, but gradually began to just float in the sling as the sedative took over.

No longer having an excuse to put it off, Keilani went to work, dreading what she would find. She located the patch of hard skin where she thought the tracking device might be. Running the transducer over Rhianna's skin around the area, she watched the images form on the corresponding screen. Her heart sank at the object that appeared. Though tiny, she was certain it shouldn't be there, and there were very few possible explanations. She stopped moving the transducer and raised her eyes to Micah's.

She saw her own despair reflected there.

"Can you remove it?" His voice was quiet, wrecked.

Keilani nodded, wanting to comfort him. No doubt he felt responsible, though Keilani knew there was no way he could watch over the animals every second. But even worse, it just confirmed there was someone on the inside involved in the drug smuggling. It was a horrific breach of trust and she sympathized with him to the depths of her being. How could anyone possibly consider betraying their family that way? Because that was how Micah would see it—utter betrayal of family.

Working carefully while Micah held the ultrasound transducer in place for her, Keilani gently prodded the tracking device from beneath Rhianna's skin. It was slow, tedious work, but Keilani didn't want to do any more damage than was absolutely necessary. Once she had it, she slid it from the cow's body and dropped it into a metal container Micah had pulled from the supply box under the ultrasound machine.

She sighed. "What next? Do you want me to go over the rest of her body with the transducer to make sure there isn't anything else? A tracking device itself doesn't exactly explain her changed behavior."

"You're the expert. But I would probably feel better if I knew there wasn't anything else." He was running his hands through his hair again, and though it was pretty short, it stood up boyishly atop his head.

She refocused her thoughts and took a deep breath. "Okay. Let's get a good look, then."

Rhianna was drifting in and out of sleep now, so she didn't protest as Keilani ran the transducer along her body, then up and down and around her fins. Nothing else seemed unusual.

Unexpectedly, Rhianna began to hiccup. It was kind of funny at first, but when it continued, the dolphin began to show obvious signs of distress. Keilani checked her vitals and found they were off. She did a vigorous search for any sign of the cause. Micah, too, was trying desperately to ascertain the problem.

"She's choking!" Keilani gasped at last. "Help me get her beak open."

He did and Keilani practically dove in, doing a thorough sweep of the depths of her throat. At first, she couldn't find anything, but finally her fingers brushed against a foreign object. She tried again to locate it in the same area, then at last, grasped it with the tips of her fingers, just firmly enough to tug it free.

Rhianna stopped her struggle almost too suddenly, but her vitals returned to normal. Micah, too, seemed to relax with relief. Or at least he did at first...until his gaze landed on what Keilani held out in the palm of her hand.

SEVEN

The obtrusive pouch filled with white powder mocked him with sickening intensity. His stomach turned over with the reality of the evil they were facing. He couldn't deny it any longer.

One of their brothers had sold them out.

Why, Lord? Why would anyone do this? He realized it was one of the first prayers he had uttered in a long time. Shame swept through him.

Keilani was saying something to him in a soft, low voice, but all he could hear was the roar of anger as the full force of the situation hit him. He shook himself, doing his best to keep his training in mind. He couldn't let it take over. He couldn't lose control. He had to keep his edge.

"Is there more?" He heard the deadly calm in his voice and knew Keilani heard it, too, when her face paled.

"Let me get a more thorough look at her abdominal cavity. It's likely there is, but I'm not sure how to extract it." To her credit, her hands didn't shake as she began probing again, but she was definitely shaken.

"Find out." He almost flinched at the harshness of

his own voice. This wasn't personal, but it was the worst betrayal he had ever felt.

Keilani reacted by performing what he asked almost mechanically. Her movements became succinct and efficient. Too efficient. He knew that was at least in part because of him. "There are a few more, that I can see."

"Will you have to cut her open?" He bit out the question.

"Maybe not. We can try some other things first."

It was a long afternoon, but thankfully, most of the rest of the world was quiet. Micah found it really odd that Keilani's attackers hadn't been around for so long. This was the longest reprieve they had gotten so far. He decided the work Keilani did with the dolphins was even more exhausting than SEAL work, at least mentally. He felt drained of everything by the time they finished with Rhianna.

"Do you think she's the only one?" Keilani's tone suggested she feared the answer.

"Probably not. But how do we figure it out? Are we going to run an ultrasound on over seventy cetaceans?" Frustration edged his voice.

"I guess not. We'll just have to keep a close eye on all of them, then." Keilani looked around the extensive property. She was probably considering the odds of figuring out which dolphins were at highest risk. And would they be able to prevent injury to them if they were being used as drug mules?

"I'd better call in the authorities to make sure these are documented and disposed of." Micah indicated the packets of drugs. He then followed her gaze. "I've decided we're staying here tonight. I'll have one of the guys bring us some food."

She surprised him with a quick response. "Good. I was thinking we should stay."

He let out a breath he hadn't known he was holding. "I was afraid you would argue. It won't be very comfortable sleeping out here."

Her response came without hesitation. "The dolphins come first."

Approval swelled within him. He shouldn't be surprised, of course, but he liked to know she was so dedicated to her calling. "What do you need from the house? I'll ask Emmett to bring it."

She pushed a lock of dark hair over her shoulder. "Nothing. I'm good."

Less than an hour later, they settled in with the food and then relaxed near the center of the dolphin facilities. Micah chose a place where they would be able to keep a good watch over the majority of the dolphins. Keilani seemed content to just observe them as they swam and played where he had turned some of them into a pen together.

"I'd like your advice on ways to improve conditions for these dolphins, if you have any to offer. There are some who think they are unjustly treated."

She seemed to choose her words carefully. "There are many who are opposed to keeping cetaceans in captivity, no matter the purpose."

"And what are your thoughts on the matter?" He watched Nikita and Mulan nose one another before splashing around.

"I believe it's a slippery slope. On one hand, dolphins and humans can get along very well. The dolphins have much to teach us. It's not very different from keeping animals in a zoo or taming wild mustangs. Do humans have the right to choose for them? I think the Bible says so, when God gave Adam the admonition to care for all the things of the earth. But how do we know when we are making good choices for them? That's the hard part." She studied her hands.

Micah was puzzling over her words. "But some might argue that wild mustangs, for example, were starving on their own. Dolphins seem to be having no trouble surviving in the wild. Does that make a difference? I'm not sure, sometimes, if we are mistreating them or not." He finally looked directly at Keilani.

"You aren't mistreating them. That's for sure. Would they be happier in the wild? Who knows? We just have to do the best we can." Her voice sounded different, strained almost.

"Yeah, I guess we are all just doing the best we can, right? So what would make life better for them, then? Other than letting them go."

"I don't know. I'll have to think about that. But they seem pretty happy and well-adjusted to me. And actually, letting them go would be difficult at this point. It would be dangerous to release them into the wild without them being reintroduced to survival skills under supervision. These dolphins no longer remember how to hunt for food and defend themselves."

"Good point. They are fed better than I am." He chuckled. She gave a small smile and looked away. He wasn't at all sure what it meant.

"In any case, at least your dolphins have a strong purpose. Defense is a little more important than putting on a show for people at an aquatic park."

She said no more, and he let it drop, but he felt sure

there had been more to the conversation than he had been aware of somehow.

It was several hours later when the hair on the back of Micah's neck began to prickle. He had just made a lap around the enclosures and settled back down beside Keilani, whom he felt sure was dozing lightly where she lay snuggled against a wall near a door. She, too, began to stir at that moment as if her senses were alerted.

A loud bang, much like a door slam, brought them both upright. Keilani started to jump up, but Micah stayed her with a hand. Then he put a finger to his lips to warn her.

They sat absolutely still, waiting. For a long time it was so quiet it was almost like they had imagined it. But just as Micah began to relax, thinking maybe the cause was something mundane he could investigate, the senses controlling his instincts buzzed awake once more. Prickles bumbled over his skin.

"Keilani, stay down. No matter what happens, just stay down." Micah rolled onto his stomach, pulling his Sig and aiming it along the horizon as he scanned the area. Nothing moved at first, but then he heard the unmistakable grind of the gate to one of the dolphin enclosures beginning to move. He dropped the gun to his side. When his eyes met Keilani's he could read the question she was silently asking him. *Do they know we're here?*

He shook his head. He wasn't positive, but he didn't think their presence had been detected. Throwing up a hand to remind her to stay put, he set his gun on the edge of the pool so he could slide himself carefully forward. He silently belly-crawled over to where the noise had seemed to originate. Just as he feared, the gate being opened was to the pen where Rhianna was normally housed. Was the perp about to discover her absence? And worse, would he grow angry when he did? Or did he already know? Was he coming because her tracker had gone dark?

Micah's main concern was for Keilani and the dolphins.

Checking over his shoulder to be sure Keilani was where he'd left her, he maneuvered himself over behind a wall to get a better look. Someone in a full-body wetsuit was bent over beside Rhianna's turnout pool peering into the water, apparently unarmed. Micah made a quick judge of distance, calculated a plan of attack in his head, then launched himself at the figure, slamming an elbow down into his back, and then cocking his fist into the man's solar plexus, momentarily stunning him. The mystery figure came up fighting, catching Micah across the jaw with a powerful punch. Micah dove at him, getting a grip on his arms and sliding him to catch him in a firm clamp around his neck. The other man responded by locking an ankle around Micah's leg and knocking them both off balance. They tumbled to the ground inches from the water, rolling away from it as each man battled to get the advantage.

Finally, Micah managed to get his forearm against the other man's throat. "Who are you?"

There was no response, only a glare of hatred from the cold blue eyes peering out from the mask. The man began to struggle again, a renewed strength throwing Micah off balance. He slipped from Micah's grip and launched himself into the water. Micah followed suit, but the perp was quickly swimming away through the gate that led to the ocean, through which he had tried to release Rhianna before discovering she was gone.

He turned back to Keilani then, only to realize she wasn't where he had left her. Had he let himself be distracted while they took her? He was berating himself before he could even form the thought.

"Keilani!" Frantic, he began searching everywhere for her. He never should have left her. He knew better.

Skidding to a halt around a corner, he heard her singsong voice call out. "Micah, it's okay. I was just checking on the patient. I'm fine."

The breath left his lungs in a rush. "Don't do that again. I told you to stay put."

He was breathing hard, trying to reconcile the terror he had just experienced with what he ought to be feeling. This wasn't his normal reaction, not to someone his only feelings toward should be professional. He had completely lost his cool, and why? The glaringly obvious answer made his stomach roll. He was developing feelings for her. It had to stop.

She was scowling at him. "You were gone a long time. I wanted to protect Rhianna in case they discovered where she was."

He raised an eyebrow and snapped out his reply. "And what were you going to do? Get both of you abducted or killed?"

She held up his Sig. "You left this behind. I thought it might be a good place to start if anyone tried."

His stomach rolled over again and a sudden feeling of incompetence swept him. He hadn't even noticed he had left his gun behind. She was affecting him in ways he never could have predicted. This just wasn't going to work. If he couldn't get it together and start acting like a trained SEAL, he would end up costing them both their lives.

Toughen up, bad boy. You're acting like a wimp. He snatched the Sig from her hand.

"Get back where you were. It's probably going to be a long night." A moment of staring at him as if she wanted to say something was all that passed. Then she wordlessly turned and went back to where he had left her earlier.

Micah watched her go, running a hand through his damp locks and trying to get a grip on his sanity. The adrenaline hadn't completely subsided and his hands shook. How was he ever going to keep this woman safe?

Keilani rolled to her side, facing away from Micah. She was still stinging from his earlier attitude and really didn't want to talk to him. Maybe if he thought she was asleep he would leave her alone with her thoughts.

She wondered, too, if she should have admitted to him that Gretchen had asked her to report back on the navy's marine mammal program on behalf of the World Animal Protection Agency. Their earlier conversation would have been a good time to tell him, but she had hesitated. Why? She wasn't really sure, other than the fact that she felt like she was betraying his trust, somehow, even though she hadn't told Gretchen anything at this point. Would he be upset to know that she had been contacted by people who believed he wasn't caring properly for his cetaceans? She shook off the question as foolish. Of course he would. Who wouldn't? She had to find a way to soften the blow somehow.

What had she gotten herself into? Taking care of military dolphins and helping out with their training had seemed like such a simple thing. She had never expected to have to protect them, nor did she expect to be in danger herself.

And Micah Kent was another matter entirely. To say that her attraction to him was complicating things was a gross understatement. He had her completely out of sorts. One minute he was tender and kind, but a second later he was barking at her again. She had no idea how to deal with it.

She should never have allowed herself to get into this situation to begin with. She had felt so sure that God was leading her to this job, but now she wondered if she had put her own desires first. Funny things happened to her insides when Micah grinned. True, that wasn't all that often, but even his steel-jawed serious expression made her feel a little flustered. Why did she always seem to have feelings for the men she knew she should stay away from?

Flashes of memory came to her of another man she had once trusted. Her stepfather—a man in uniform who should have protected her...

"Keilani." Micah spoke softly behind her.

She half rolled to face him and found he was close— too close. She could smell a faint hint of his soap and something else unique to the man. There was a tiny dimple nestled in his cheek and she fought the urge to place her finger there.

"Lights." He pointed. "We need to go see what's going on. But I'm not leaving you again."

She looked in the direction he indicated. She saw shadows moving in the distance, barely discernable in the dark. Keilani and Micah were sheltered by a wall on two sides, but there was an open area beyond, leading out to the enclosures jutting into the bay. She couldn't tell if the shadows were along the outer runners and walkways or farther beyond.

"Do you think they are looking for Rhianna?" She sat fully up, no longer at all sleepy. The thought that dangerous and angry men might be coming for the sweet girl made her stomach flop.

"There's a good possibility. But the other possibility is that—"

"They're coming for me." She finished his sentence flatly.

"Yeah." He looked at her for a long moment. He didn't have to say what he was feeling, because she could see it in his eyes. He would protect her with his very life. "I guess there's one way to find out."

Keeping to the shadows, Keilani and Micah made their way to the far end of the pens where they had seen the lights. Somewhere in the interim the lights had disappeared. She kept searching, but Keilani never saw them again. She wanted to ask Micah, but she didn't want to give up their position.

As if he knew her thoughts, he pointed. Following his indication, she saw two shadows moving carefully along the walkway only a few feet away now. He put a finger to his lips as she looked back toward him. She nodded and he indicated for her to stay there, just before he was gone.

In a flash Micah had disoriented one man and tossed the other into the water. He wrestled his way out and came back for Micah, however, and they engaged in hand-to-hand combat once more. Keilani watched helplessly, struggling to keep quiet and remain where she was. What if the other guy came to again? Could Micah fight them both off?

As a SEAL, his combat skills were very impressive, but this other guy could certainly hold his own also. Coincidence because he was a hardened criminal, or was he also a SEAL? She didn't really know what to think.

It seemed to go on and on. Every time she thought Micah had the advantage, the masked man turned the fight to his benefit once more. She wanted to cry out in frustration and when the unconscious man began to stir, too, she debated on trying to help. How would he manage? Did he even realize the second man was waking up?

She was just about to call out to warn him when Micah flung the man he was fighting into the feet of the second man just as he began to stand. The man tumbled into the water on the ocean side, where the enclosures ended and security was lessened because the depth of the ocean made it much more difficult to get to, but the first man stood and came back at Micah in a rage. Micah used the man's ire against him, however, and soon had him pinned and an arm securely wound around his neck.

Keilani had no time to celebrate his victory, however, before the cold steel of a pistol butt made contact with her temple. A scream burst out a nanosecond before a hand covered her mouth.

She watched Micah's grip falter and almost lose his hold on his opponent when he looked up to see the third man holding a gun to her head.

Keilani tried to communicate to him with her eyes. *I didn't move this time. I promise.*

She could see the indecision, the playing of his options running through his head. He was smart and tough, but he was outplayed. Surely, he could see that. Outplayed and outnumbered.

He began to relax his grip.

"That's right. Let my friend go and I won't shoot her just yet." The voice in Keilani's ear was raspy and despicable.

She couldn't quite suppress the whimper in her throat. She knew she was going to die either way. If he let his man go, it would only prolong the inevitable. How could she convince him to hold on?

The thought crossed her mind that maybe she could attempt to get away. Even if he shot her now, it would give Micah the chance to even the score. He could get his man and save the dolphins. It would be worth the risk.

He shook his head at her. She didn't know if he actually understood what she was thinking but she took it as a sign. Did he have a plan?

She waited a few more seconds. Micah didn't move and the man jerked her up tighter, beginning to grow impatient.

"I said let him go!"

The man Micah held was grappling at his hand and struggling against him, but Micah had a steel grip on him. "How do I know you won't just shoot her anyway?"

He was buying time. What was he waiting on?

"You don't. But maybe if you let him go, I'll wait and you won't have to watch. She might be fun to keep alive a little longer anyway." He shrugged, but the effect was lost because of his lingering anger.

Micah's eyes narrowed but there was no other indication of how the man's words affected him. Keilani felt sure he was furious under that calm facade. He would never let his opponent know it, though.

Then, out of nowhere, he just slackened his grip and the man dropped to the floor, unconscious. Keilani stared in awe, looking from the man on the ground to Micah and back. He had known exactly what he was doing, down to the second the man would pass out. The man still holding the gun to her head was trembling. He realized it, too.

"Let her go." Micah stepped over the downed man and began to stalk toward them, a hunter coming for his prey.

"I'll shoot her. Stop right there."

Micah stopped, but feral confidence oozed from his stance. "No, I don't think you will."

He half turned, nonchalant in his manner, and when the other man slackened his grip to analyze this odd move, Keilani instantly relaxed every muscle in her body, dragging them down to the ground. The masked man released her, not expecting her full weight to fall on him, and Micah kicked the gun from his hand in one lightning-fast motion.

Keilani rolled out of the way as Micah dove for her assailant, then she slid toward the gun, just in case. The metal grip still warm from her attacker's hand repulsed her and she had to focus to keep from dropping it. The briny scent of ocean water mingled with sweat from the struggling men and she felt sick, even as a cool breeze wafted over her.

Micah wasted little time overpowering the weaker man and soon he, too, was unconscious. "Call for help and I'll secure them."

Keilani did as he asked, but while he tied the man who had taken Keilani hostage, she realized the other unconscious man wasn't where Micah had left him.

"Micah, the other man." She pointed.

He muttered something unintelligible. "Stay here."

She would rather go with Micah than stay with the tied-up man on the walkway, but she didn't protest.

A few minutes later he returned, his hand standing his thick, dark hair on end again. She knew what he was going to say before the words came. "He's gone."

EIGHT

Micah didn't expect to gain anything from the man they had captured, but when they found out he was a former SEAL-in-training kicked out of the program for suspected involvement in illegal activities, it was the first real break they had gotten.

David Schmidt had reportedly been involved in selling and smuggling illegal substances over four years ago. But that didn't explain the link he had now, though he had been stationed here at one time. That explained how he knew his way around.

As for the two men who had escaped, the captured man wouldn't give up their identities. For some reason Micah felt at least one of them was the key to unraveling this puzzle.

His worry for Keilani intensified. It seemed the men after her were professionals, at least in part. While he might be prepared to deal with whatever they threw at him personally, he had to be more careful not to leave Keilani vulnerable. In truth, he was still annoyed with himself for letting the man get his hands on her.

The dolphins, of course, were another worry. He had to figure out how these men were getting access to his mammals and make sure it never happened again. Tightening security from the ocean side of the enclosures seemed to be the first order of the day.

It was past time to investigate the site where Keilani had first seen the divers. In fact, Micah didn't want to wait a moment longer. He would love to make the dive without Keilani because of the danger, but leaving her unprotected while he explored the deep wasn't a good idea. Xavier would have to guard her.

When he explained this to her, she protested. They had already loaded the boat and were making their way across the bay.

"Oh, no." She was looking at him intently. "Please don't tell me you still intend to make me stay on the boat."

He tried to fight back the grimace. He was pretty sure it didn't work. "I think it would be best. We've talked about this already."

"Actually, you talked. I think you might need my help to find the spot." She almost looked a little smug as she made the announcement—as if she knew she had a valid argument. Which she did...

"It can't be that difficult to find." He tilted his head and frowned at her.

"Then how have they kept it secret all this time?" She was still giving him that look. The boat had stopped moving and they were idling in the bay.

He glanced away. "If it's so hard to find, how did you see the hiding place for the crate?"

She shrugged, her expression relaxing. "I wasn't looking for it. At first I didn't even realize where they were."

He still wasn't convinced. "And you think I can't possibly find it without you?"

"Maybe you could. But wouldn't it be faster if I just show you? It's under the water and I would be able to point it out easier if I were with you. It isn't discernable from the surface. We shouldn't waste any more time." She knew she was winning.

"It's true we really don't have time to waste." He hated to give in, but arguing about it was only wasting more time.

"I'll stay close. You already know I'm a good swimmer."

"All right, then. Are you familiar with scuba gear?" He didn't look up. People were supposed to have training before going on a dive. He didn't know what he would do if she didn't know how to dive.

"I've been diving before, yes. I can manage." Her steady gaze drew his eyes up to hers.

He let out the breath he'd been holding. "Good. Let's see if we can gather you some gear and get going."

Xavier and Emmett met them at the dock and they took a local friend's boat out to the approximate location where Keilani saw the other boat. They didn't dare take a SEAL RHIB boat out without permission from the navy, and Micah wasn't about to wait around on the go-ahead. There was no sign of any activity around the site now, and if that changed, Xavier would use his skill as a highly trained sniper to take out any enemy who might approach from the top side. Micah would lead the way with Keilani sandwiched between him and Emmett below the surface. He would rather have it the other way around, but he would trust Emmett with his life, so he could trust him to have Keilani's six today. He needed to be in front so he could spot any danger below without Keilani being in the line of sight. He was bigger than Emmett and it would be easier for Micah to signal Keilani to go back if he was in front of her.

The California sun shone yellow and white across the crystal-blue waters, deceptive in the picture of serenity it painted. Gentle waves lapped at the sides of the boat as the trio prepared to launch their mission. Keilani described what she could remember to the men as they prepped to dive.

"I hope we don't have to spend much time under there." Keilani was speaking close to his ear. "I've never really liked diving with scuba gear. I prefer to swim free or just snorkel. But there is no way I can just sit on the boat and hope you find it."

It wasn't the first time he had noticed her dislike of feeling closed in, and he wondered at the reasons for her claustrophobia.

"I'll be right there if you need me. We will try to get it over quickly." Micah touched her arm lightly, then wished he hadn't when the electric current shot through him again. She smiled in gratitude, though.

"Let's go." Micah realized that Emmett was watching them again, trying not to make it obvious. He was going to have to set his friend straight. Emmett seemed to think there was something going on between Keilani and Micah.

He put it out of his mind and they hit the water, keeping to the plan as Keilani motioned them in the right direction. The water ebbed around them, turning the world surreal, shrouded in a transparent blue cloud. It was amazingly clear, also very cold, and Micah never ceased to be impressed by the magic of it all. He could see far into the depths, taking in every detail of the bottom and the sea life around them. Sharks would be a concern, but so far there were none nearby.

They soon reached the area where Keilani had seen the divers, and upon close inspection, they found evidence that someone had recently been there. The reef was empty of sea life and some of the sediment from the bottom of the sea floor was still floating around where it had been stirred up. However, the reef contained nothing out of the ordinary, just a few startled fish.

Keilani looked at Micah and shrugged. Emmett gestured for them to wait. As they watched, he swam in close and began to touch parts of the reef. He manipulated a piece here and there until a whole chunk came loose. It was fake. There, beneath the missing piece of artificial reef, lay a hollowed-out section of ocean floor, two metal cases nestled carefully inside. Micah had a pretty good idea what they would find in the cases.

Taking out his waterproof phone, he snapped a few pictures, opened the cases, and when the bags of white powder secured in waterproof plastic appeared, he took more pictures of those.

He gestured for Emmett to leave the cases. They made sure the missing piece of reef was secured back into place before slowly surfacing. He took no chances on Keilani getting the bends, even though they weren't really diving very deep.

When they surfaced, Emmett began to question Micah. "You just plan to leave them down there?"

"I'll report what we have found to the United States Navy and let the investigation team work out the retrieval. They need to know where the drug runners are operating from. And if we take their goods, they will know we are on to them. " He began to swim back to the boat.

"Does that mean we'll have to come back?" Keilani looked a little sickened at the thought. The idea of running into the drug runners probably didn't set well, and the more time they spent down there, the more likely they would get caught.

"No need for that. I saved the coordinates." He gestured to his wrist where he wore a high-tech watch and saw her face relax a little.

The roar of a boat motor put his senses on alert, however, and when he scanned the horizon, it was headed straight for them. The trio was still a good swim from their own boat, which had drifted a good distance away with the ocean's tide, and the new vessel was moving at a high speed.

He called out to Keilani, but her wide-eyed gaze was already fixed on the oncoming speedboat. She looked frozen with fear, prompting Micah to swim to her. Xavier had started toward them in the boat, and Emmett, too, closed in around Keilani. If they went down, it would be together. That was what SEAL family was for.

"Get your gear in place," Micah instructed Keilani with a calm tone. "We may have to dive to avoid the boat."

Her nervous gaze darted between him and the speedboat as she swallowed and nodded. She followed his instructions as he and Emmett did the same.

They were exactly halfway between the two boats, which now seemed to be headed directly for one another. When Xavier would alter his course to avoid the nose of the other boat, it would change course as well, keeping the bow pointed right at Xavier. They were closing in and it wasn't going to be pretty.

"On the count of three, we dive and go as deep as we can as fast as we can. I'll let you know when we can surface again." Micah waited for acknowledgment and then began to count down while locking hands with them both.

The trio dove with all their might, Micah and Emmett practically dragging Keilani along between them, though she kicked as hard as she could. It was only a matter of seconds before a blast rocked the surface and hot water pushed them toward the ocean floor on a forceful current. The surface of the water brightened above them and then dimmed to a dull orange glow. A few bits of debris were projected through the water around them. Somewhere to their far right, Micah caught a glimpse of Xavier's form as it launched into the depths. He had made it off the boat in time.

Micah kept an eye out for the other boat driver. He, too, had probably hit the water before the collision. Now they would all have to swim back to the beach.

He thought about Keilani's arrival and wondered if she was experiencing a sense of déjà vu right now. She was going to wish she had never taken this job.

The water slowly quieted above them and Micah, Keilani and Emmett began to drift back to the surface. Micah steered them as much toward the beach as he could, all the while keeping a lookout for both Xavier and the other boat driver and making sure Keilani stayed within easy reach.

Before they could break the surface, however, a projectile shot through the water toward them. Micah lunged for Keilani in slow motion under the water, pulling her back into the depths as the underwater missile missed her by inches, exploding into a small section of reef thirty feet away. Apparently the boat driver hadn't been operating alone. Was there another enemy boat nearby? Where else could they be shooting the torpedoes from?

Micah could see Keilani's wide eyes behind her mask, and he prodded her into action. He had no idea where their attacker was, only an approximate direction. It was only seconds before another missile appeared. Avoiding contact by a fraction of an inch, they began to swim frantically back toward the shore.

Micah had lost track of both Xavier and Emmett but knew his brothers could easily take care of themselves. It was up to him to protect Keilani.

He did have to admire her physical strength, though. She was more than just a strong swimmer—she was a powerful athlete, cutting through the water with amazing strength.

The fact did nothing to make him feel better about the constant barrage of torpedoes, however. It took far too much energy to avoid the projectiles, slowing them down much more than he would have liked. Keilani adapted with grace, bobbing and rising in the water at the onset of each new obstacle like one of the dolphins playing a new game. He could see that she was growing fatigued.

The ocean floor below them gradually grew shallower, granting a bit of hope, but just as Micah began to believe they might actually make it, the ominous shadow of a shark fell over them. It was relatively small, but still just as threatening. Keilani practically froze in the water—not the reaction he had expected from her. He tried to urge her on, but she was unresponsive.

The shark hadn't yet noticed them, but he was directly in their path to shore. They could swim around him and risk expending energy they might not be able to afford, or they could try distracting him long enough to swim past. He couldn't do either, if he couldn't get Keilani moving.

She seemed frozen in place in the water, as if some sudden arctic blast had frozen her into a solid object. But she was prodded into action as the huge beast swung his beady eyes toward them.

Micah was left without a choice as the shark began to charge. Without hesitation, he motioned for Keilani to go while he moved forward to distract the shark. The animal started, then swung back toward Keilani, her smaller size evidently indicating an easier meal.

Diving toward it, Micah grabbed the huge shark's dorsal fin, seeking to anger it in hopes of granting Keilani time to escape. The shark arched toward Micah, massive jaws wide in attack.

Micah jetted upward in the water, the shark's teeth barely missing his foot. Diving once more, he watched Keilani pass as he floated a moment to attract the shark's attention. This time when the shark sped in for the kill, Micah drove toward it, driving all of the force he could through his feet and connecting with the top of the shark's head, momentarily stunning it. While the shark writhed in surprise, Micah used all the energy he had left to follow Keilani toward the shore.

Fatigue weighed on him, pulling his middle down and tugging at his legs. The temptation to just stop swimming and let the fatigue win hit him hard. He could see Keilani up ahead, looking back and urging him on but it was in a delayed motion, his body retreating into a dreamlike state. But SEAL training had taught him exactly how to deal with this.

Focusing with every ounce of his strength, he forced his way out of his own head. With fierce strokes, he powered toward Keilani, giving no quarter as he snatched her around the waist and drove them toward the shore.

The shark had lost interest since its meal turned out to be more difficult than it had anticipated, but the torpedoes kept coming. He could tell Keilani was getting tired. Her motions had slowed considerably and he feared one of the torpedoes might strike her. They were small, but he had seen what kind of damage the projectiles could cause. Designed to explode on impact, they easily caused serious damage, sometimes death, to their victims.

The shore still seemed an infinite distance away, but he kept them moving. A shadow darkened the water above him, and Micah tried to determine if the hull of the boat was friend or foe. He was almost certain it was a fishing boat, which did nothing to answer his question. Keilani looked up and pointed, but he could only shrug and urge her on.

Keilani's adrenaline had run out and it had taken her strength with it. The seawater grew warmer as they got closer to shore, but it wasn't helping her morale any. The urge to quit swimming was so strong now that she was having to try to think of other things. The diving gear only weighed her down more, and she had no hope of keeping up with Micah's superior athleticism.

His tug on her hand urged her a little faster for a bit, but he had to be growing frustrated with her. In an effort not to disappoint him, she dug deep and gave a renewed push. Each torpedo was harder to dodge, but they weren't coming as frequently as before.

Keilani worried about Emmett and Xavier, though. They were well trained for this type of adventure, but she hadn't seen them for so long that it concerned her. The boat hull above them had moved on, but now it seemed to be cruising back in their direction. It slowed, not far above them, and a diver hit the water.

Keilani's heart plunged into a rapid rhythm once more. Was it another enemy swimmer intending to finish them off? She couldn't tell, but the diver had definitely spotted them and now swam in their direction.

Micah stiffened, but then the other diver gave some sort of signal and he relaxed, tugging Keilani toward the boat. He helped her aboard and she slumped onto the deck in absolute exhaustion. She was relieved to find that the other diver was Emmett.

Micah stripped off his scuba gear as he began talking rapidly with the other diver, as well as another man on the boat. Xavier was there, too, she realized. He must have found the fishing boat and come looking for her and Micah after finding Emmett. She was too spent from the long swim to have more than a passing interest right now, though. She probably would have been content to lay facedown on the boat deck had Micah not come to check on her.

"Are you okay? Are you hurt anywhere?" He gently rolled her over.

Keilani suppressed a groan. "I'm fine, just so very exhausted."

A stranger handed her a bottle of water and a towel. She thanked him as Micah introduced him as a local fisherman. Tom Hawkins had apparently witnessed the boat crash and rescued Xavier right away. They had easily found Emmett after he shot back to the surface, but it had taken them a little longer to locate Micah and Keilani.

"Do you know anything at all about what happened to the driver of the other boat?" Micah was speaking to the boat captain.

"I saw him jump right before the collision, but couldn't find him by the time I picked up Petty Officer Carraway here." He gestured to Xavier but shook his head. "It's like he just disappeared. As for the torpedoes, I assume he had an accomplice. He probably had him staked out keeping watch."

"Did you happen to get a good look at the man on the other boat? Could the torpedo guy have come from the same boat? Do you think he had more than one guy helping him?" Micah fixed Tom with an intimidating stare, but the fisherman just blinked back at him, friendly expression never wavering.

"No. There was only one more and the fella driving the boat had on a wetsuit, like maybe he knew he'd be swimming. Maybe they were both involved with the torpedoes somehow, too. It could have been there was a second boat that I didn't see. They had to be getting the torpedoes somewhere. Who can say?" Tom handed Micah a bottle of water. "The boat looked familiar, though. I've seen it a few times in these waters."

Xavier let out a snort. "Guess you won't be seeing it again."

Tom just nodded. "It was a strange choice for the bay

here. Not any of the rentals. A high-dollar speedboat. Not practical, but most folks around here who want to show off just buy a yacht."

"Unless it had another purpose. Maybe they wanted something fast?" Micah was fishing for information now. Keilani pulled the towel closer around her as the chill of shock set in.

"Oh, I've heard the rumors. I try to mind my own business, but people talk. You're wanting to know if I think it has something to do with the drug runners rumored to be in the area?" Tom cocked an eyebrow at him.

"Do you?" Micah took a gulp from his water bottle.

"Hard to say. Suspicion alone can get a man killed in a deal like that." Tom turned away.

"Just a minute, Mr. Hawkins." Micah stopped him. "If the rumors are that prevalent, why has the press not made any mention of it?"

Tom pulled at his beard. "Don't imagine they want any part of the cartel's wrath, either."

He walked away and Micah turned back to Keilani. "This is bigger than I thought."

Keilani nodded. "But the biggest question I have is how involved are your dolphins?" The creases on his forehead did nothing to console her.

His lips compressed into a thin white line. "I don't know, but they chose the wrong dolphins to mess with."

He stalked away, obviously too angry to talk about it. His body language suggested he was struggling to keep calm, so she let him go without comment.

Truthfully, it angered her, as well. The mere idea of ruthless drug smugglers using innocent mammals in such a horrific way made her want to lash out, too.

And Micah probably felt responsible. She honestly had no clue how anyone could manage to get their hands on navy sea mammals under the radar. It seemed impossible despite the ease with which these men seemed to be coming and going. They had to have knowledge of the whole layout of the dolphin enclosures, but it should be better protected, even top secret. She didn't like where all the evidence was pointing.

A few minutes later she was still standing where Micah had left her when Tom Hawkins returned. He offered her a sandwich and she accepted gratefully. It would help to settle her nerves and replenish her energy.

"I understand you're a doctor?" The seaman asked Keilani the question as if the prospect scared him. She found that odd.

"I'm actually a veterinarian. I'm here as a consultant for the navy sea mammal program." Keilani watched his face, and he relaxed some when she explained.

"Oh. I wondered what a doctor would be doing out here with a bunch of navy SEALs. But Xavier called you Dr. Lucas. A vet—that makes more sense." He was rubbing his beard again and she wasn't sure if it was a nervous habit or just something he did when he was thinking. There was something vaguely familiar about him, though.

"Did you just happen upon the boat crash? We're fortunate you were around." Keilani took another sip from her water bottle.

"Not exactly. I was nearby, but Xavier radioed me. You see, he's my nephew. He knew I'd be somewhere around and that you all were in danger." His nonchalant tone suggested he was accustomed to his nephew being in danger. The fact that he was Xavier's uncle might be why he seemed familiar, too.

"Well, I'm very thankful you were." Keilani offered him a smile. He just nodded in return.

Before anything else could be said, Emmett sat down beside her. "Dr. Lucas, there's one more thing. I wanted to make sure you were recovered first, but we urgently need your help. We found a seriously wounded dolphin on the dive and managed to haul him in."

"What? Where is he? We need to get him to the veterinary facilities immediately." She rose, finding a surge of adrenaline she didn't know she had left.

Emmett put a hand on her arm. "He's in the stern in a tub the captain used for fishing. We've rigged up a temporary sling for him. Come on and I'll show you."

NINE

As they situated the new patient in the care unit at the base, Keilani couldn't hold back her tears. It was one thing for someone to come after her, but anyone who could harm an innocent dolphin was a monster. Micah was watching her, so she fought to get it under control. This little guy needed her help.

She uttered a quiet prayer as she ran her hands along the dolphin's sleek form, careful not to cause him any additional pain.

Micah watched silently while she prayed over the dolphin. His voice was quiet with what she could only label reverence when she finished. "Do you think he's going to be okay? Can you get him back to health?"

"We." She turned to him. "I think *we* can. I need your help."

Xavier and Emmett had helped them get the sea mammal settled, but once they were sure there was nothing more they could do, the pair went to complete reports on the day's misadventure.

She began to give instructions, even as she assessed the mammal's wounds. They soon had him sedated and on IV fluids, with several monitors extending from his form to keep tabs on his vitals. He had apparently been restrained and abused, his wounds indicative of someone's anger. It was a wonder the poor guy trusted any humans to get near him. That fact alone was a testament to his weakened condition and the pain he was suffering.

Keilani began by giving him something for the pain and treating the external wounds, but the damage went below the surface. She used the sonogram machine next to determine how extensive the internal injuries were. After a thorough examination with the device, she declared him very fortunate.

"It doesn't appear to have caused him any major trauma to his internal organs. We should be able to see him healthy again in a week or so." She gave Micah a teary look.

"This isn't your fault, Keilani." He put a hand on her shoulder.

"Of course it is. It's a message. Someone wants me to back off." She turned away.

"You can't blame yourself. These men—they're just ruthless. And besides, you're going to help him." His expression brooked no argument.

Keilani nodded. "He's going to be okay. But he should never have had to go through this."

"That's true, but one thing SEAL life has taught me is that there are evil men in the world and we can't shoulder the responsibility for their actions. Their choices are sometimes intolerable, but those choices are theirs alone. All we can do is try to prevent them from hurting anyone or anything else the best we can." The steely-jawed expression she was becoming familiar with was back on his face. "And what you can do is help me make sure they are caught so this never happens again."

She could only nod at him in reply. Her throat was too thick with emotion to squeeze any words past.

They continued to work with the dolphin, named Gus, for another couple of hours without a break.

Even as they sat at Gus's metaphorical bedside, Keilani wondered about how her attacker kept managing to elude them. No matter where they were or what the situation was, the wet-suit clad figure always seemed to disappear into thin air. The one guy that always seemed to be involved was the one they could never catch. She knew it was the same man because of his build and mannerisms.

"It's like he's a ghost." Keilani hadn't meant to speak the words aloud, but for once she was glad for the slipup, because Micah was looking at her like she had just solved a riddle.

"You might be onto something." He pulled out his phone and did a web search without further comment. She watched him until finally he showed her an article.

"Navy SEAL subgroup known as Ghosts infiltrate a top-secret enemy organization in Afghanistan." Keilani read the first line aloud, then looked back at Micah. "Would any of those men have been stationed here?"

"I'll have to see what I can find out. The names of the men should be in military records. I'll have my friend on the investigation team see what he can find out." Micah sent a quick text to Paul, including the article link and explaining his theory.

It was several minutes later that Micah received a text telling him that Paul would see what he could find and send him the information in an email. The waiting was brutal, but finally he got an email with some photos, names and a little bit more information.

"It doesn't look like any of them are still active. But one man used to be stationed here. We just need to find out where that man is now." He brought up a picture and enlarged it.

Keilani looked it over. "Bax Jarnigan? Wow, that's a unique name." Keilani shook her head. "And he looks… well, frightening, to say the least."

"Some former SEALs have trouble moving on after active duty. They've seen things and it's hard to get over. But it doesn't explain how he could still have such complete access to the facilities." Micah kept searching.

"You think he's working with someone who's still active now?" Keilani peeked over his shoulder.

"As much as I want to deny it, I'm afraid it's very likely. I don't know how else to explain it. Even a former Ghost couldn't get complete access like your attacker has done. He knows how to breach the walls around the outside of the dolphin enclosure, he has no trouble accessing the security footage and he always knows where we are." Micah kept searching. "We just have to find the link."

The sound of someone coming in the door of the marine mammal care unit drew their attention. A man Keilani vaguely recognized from seeing him once or twice around the base stuck his head in. Micah tensed.

"Lieutenant Kent, your presence is requested in the admiral's office." The officer looked Keilani over with a blank expression.

"What for? This dolphin is in critical condition." His annoyance was apparent in his stance.

The other officer shrugged. "Something about the

incident today. Can't Dr. Lucas take care of the dolphin? Isn't that why she's here?" His eyes narrowed for a split second, but he recovered so quickly she thought she'd imagined it.

"She's under protection and shouldn't be left alone." Micah cut her a strange look. She couldn't be sure what he was thinking, but his hackles were definitely up. "Someone will have to relieve me first. Someone I trust."

"Take it up with the admiral." The man ducked back out the door.

"Does he always have that mammoth chip on his shoulder?" Keilani made a face.

"More so lately." Micah frowned, clearly musing over the thought. "Petty Officer Taggert has been through a rough time, though. His family has been struggling, and I think his wife has just left him. He's never told any of us for sure, just distanced himself. I try to give him plenty of space until he's ready to talk or move on. He seems to be handling it well most days, but we are all afraid he might be a little volatile."

"I would, too. But hey, if you need to see what this is all about, I'll be fine by myself here with Gus for a little while. It seems safer now that the admiral has increased security." Keilani adjusted the line on the dolphin's IV.

Micah scoffed. "No way. If the admiral wants me to sit in on this meeting right now he'll have to send someone else to stay with you. Someone I trust."

No one else came, though, and Keilani grew more suspicious as time passed. "Do you think it was just some kind of ploy to separate us?"

Micah shook his head. "I had the same thought, so I sent a text to Emmett. He confirmed that the admiral asked for me, but he also had no idea about Gus at the time. He had just assumed you'd be coming with me. I didn't know you were thinking the same thing, though."

It was only a few minutes later when the admiral himself walked in. The men exchanged salutes. "How's the patient, Dr. Lucas?" He stopped beside the care unit and peered in at the dolphin. His eyes widened when he saw the full extent of the animal's wounds.

"He's doing okay, but it's a bit touch and go still. As long as he doesn't worsen overnight, he should improve greatly by tomorrow." Keilani began to explain the extent of his treatment.

When she had finished, the admiral nodded. "I'm sure you're doing a fine job. I just want you to know we are increasing the guard around the dolphins to keep a closer eye on them. Apparently, our earlier efforts were insufficient. I have some surveillance specialists checking out the feed for loops. I intend to see these men stopped right away and we will do whatever is necessary to apprehend them."

He didn't go into great detail about the operation, but Keilani felt confident he wanted it over just as much as she did. Once again she was reassured that the rumors of the navy mistreating its animals were entirely fabricated.

When he left, Micah squinted at her. "The admiral likes you. That's quite a compliment. He doesn't like many people." Then he winked.

Keilani felt her cheeks warm. "Why would you say that? That he likes me, I mean."

"He complimented you. And he went to the trouble of telling you about his plans. The admiral doesn't explain himself to anyone." He turned back to the dolphin. "So he's still pretty critical?"

Keilani nodded. "His vitals are fluctuating. He just isn't very stable. I won't feel confident in his ability to fully recover before tomorrow anyway."

"Keilani, tell me why you are so nervous around anyone in a military uniform. I noticed you eyeing all the insignias on Admiral McLeary's uniform. But it isn't just high-ranking officers that bother you, is it? Does it have something to do with your fear of small spaces?" He dropped down beside her in a chair.

The unexpected question caught her completely off guard. "How did you know? I mean, I thought I was getting better—about concealing it, at least."

"You withdraw, almost imperceptibly, but there is a stiffness to your demeanor when anyone in a uniform gets close. I've noticed you are more relaxed around me when I'm not in uniform, and it isn't just naval officers. You did the same with the police."

Keilani was quiet, not wanting to open up, yet knowing she owed him something. Maybe she could tell him enough to satisfy his curiosity. "It was my stepfather. He's the reason I eventually moved in with my grandparents."

"He was in the military?" Micah's eyes softened, all the invitation she needed to capitulate.

"Yes. The air force. And he was ruthless, both at home and in the service. I eventually learned he had been discharged under questionable circumstances." Keilani winced, hating the guilt that swamped her at the satisfaction she felt at the thought that he had gotten what he deserved.

"When you say he was ruthless…"

She closed her eyes, letting out a small burst of breath before she continued. "He abused me. He beat my mother first and I tried to intervene. He used his fists to convince me their relationship was none of my affair." Keilani shuddered at the memory of his merciless beatings. "He took great pleasure in locking me in small spaces for hours at a time. I eventually learned how to get out. It was like a game to him to see if I could escape each new trap he put me in. One day I escaped an especially terrifying dark space and I decided somehow I would just have to get out for good."

"How did you manage to get away?"

"I tried to convince my mother to leave for years, but she wouldn't. I finally decided after that particularly frightening ordeal, preceded by a brutal beating, I had to leave without her. She would have to make the decision on her own. I snuck out late one night while he was in a deep sleep, probably drug induced, I realized later. I managed to contact my grandparents, and they came to get me and took me in." Keilani bit her lip. "He wanted to come after me when he found out where I was, but my grandfather threatened to press charges if he did, so he backed down."

"Did your mother ever get out?" Micah looked as if he already knew the answer.

"No. Last I heard she was still with him. I've lost all contact with her now."

Micah struggled to digest all that Keilani had just revealed. No wonder she didn't like feeling confined. His stomach turned over at the thought of Keilani's mother living with the constant abuse as well as losing all contact with such an amazing daughter. But Keilani was right. She couldn't force her mother to make the decision to leave.

"How old were you when your mother married this man?" He had to wonder how much this had affected her life.

"I was ten. I managed to escape and go live with my grandparents at thirteen." She blinked at him. "I tried for years to keep in contact with my mother. He forbade it until I graduated from veterinary school."

"He was interested in you reentering their lives once you could contribute something to him." Micah scowled.

"Exactly. Since then it has been my choice not to connect with her." Keilani tried to keep him from seeing the pain in her eyes by lowering her lids. He didn't miss it, though. She regretted cutting her mother out of her life.

"What happened to your biological father?"

When she winced, Micah wanted to take back his question. "I'm sorry. I'm asking too much of you."

"No, no. It's okay. He chose not to be a part of my life. He left my mom when I was around four years old. I have only seen him three or four times since." Her voice broke.

"Wow. That was really dumb on his part. That must have been tough growing up." Micah wanted to take her in his arms when her face crumpled, but he didn't dare risk it. Already, she was getting under his skin. He couldn't take a chance on her burrowing in even deeper. It was already going to be difficult on them both to part ways when the time came.

Her nod finally registered in his brain and he tried

to construct a reply. But his throat was tight, and he wasn't sure how to offer the appropriate condolences.

She saved him just in time. "When my stepfather used his fists on me he was usually in uniform, so the sight of it gradually became conditioned in my mind as a warning of imminent danger. And then his son, who was quite a bit older than me and also in the military, followed in his footsteps when it came to mistreating me, so it only worsened matters."

"You had a stepbrother?"

"Yes, and he was horrible. Fortunately, he didn't live with us long, but I had suffered enough trauma by the time he moved out that it stuck with me."

Before Micah could reply, one of the sensors monitoring the dolphin's vitals began to emit a series of high-pitched beeps. Keilani quickly began to check the monitors as Micah moved closer to Gus to see how the dolphin was looking. Gus was completely motionless.

"His blood pressure is dropping. His temp is lower than normal, as well. We've got to get him stabilized." Keilani began working on her patient with quick, efficient movements. "He's going into shock."

"What can I do?" Micah felt helpless, not a feeling he dealt well with.

She instructed him on how to increase the dolphin's IV fluids while she administered norepinephrine. The treatment tank was equipped with a heating apparatus, and Keilani asked him to increase the temperature. The dolphin remained unresponsive, but Keilani didn't give up. Micah watched her, amazed, as she calmly continued to work on the dolphin, taking action almost by instinct, until at last he started to show some slight signs of improvement. He breathed a sigh of relief when Gus's vitals began to normalize.

"He's going to have a rough night." Keilani readjusted some of the wires attached to the monitoring equipment.

"Poor little guy. He's fortunate to have you." Micah tried not to lock eyes with her, but couldn't help it. Surely, she would see that the dolphin wasn't the only one he felt was fortunate to have her right now. Even so, he couldn't let her get the wrong idea. He still planned to remain single after what had happened with Jade. He had been ready to give up his career for her before she betrayed him. That would have been a huge mistake. So it was better that neither of them get attached in any way.

"I don't know that I can help him enough to save him." Keilani's eyes spoke many things her words did not. "We'll just have to wait and see. He's experienced some shock and lost a lot of blood."

Micah could tell Keilani was fading fast. It was somewhere in the neighborhood of 2:00 a.m. and they had experienced three more scares with Gus, taking every bit of energy they had left. As if the unplanned swim hadn't been enough to physically exhaust them, Gus's condition took a mental and emotional toll, as well. Combine that with the recent drain on their adrenaline supplies and it was a recipe for complete exhaustion—something Micah had been trained to overcome, but Keilani had not. He didn't know how she was still functioning.

This was the ideal time for the enemy to strike. Knowing that, he upped his own mental game. SEAL training had taught him to fight mental exhaustion as well as physical exhaustion. It was the only way SEALs could do their job. He would need to protect Keilani right now more than ever.

She was fighting to remain alert. Micah wasn't about to relax his vigil, so he offered her the opportunity to rest. "Keilani, why don't you sleep for a little while. I can wake you if anything comes up with Gus. He seems to be doing okay for now."

He almost expected her to protest, so he was relieved when she agreed. "That sounds wonderful, actually. Are you sure you don't mind?"

"No. You need your strength. No telling what tomorrow will bring. Until we catch these guys…" He trailed off, wishing he hadn't brought it up again. He wanted her to rest, not worry.

"You're right." She had stiffened somewhat. "Wake me if you need me."

She was asleep almost immediately and he was alone with his thoughts. It was a dangerous place to be, considering the vulnerable way her face relaxed into sleep.

He shut out thoughts of Keilani and his attraction to her. He needed to focus on protecting her and apprehending her attacker right now. He had considered every possibility, but he still came up short on answers. No one on their team seemed capable of betraying him this way. True, SEALs learned to be the toughest and most hardened breed of men in times of battle, but they were not without honor by any means. That honor began with loyalty to country and their brothers, so walking around base like nothing was wrong while aiding and abetting smugglers and trying to kill innocent people was inconceivable.

Micah mulled over every single man in the unit. Of course Emmett and Xavier could be dismissed from suspicion, not because they were his roommates and best friends, but because they had been with him and Keilani during nearly every attack.

He knew if he could find anyone with a link to Bax Jarnigan and the Ghosts he would probably have his man, but the truth was, a link like that was hard to pinpoint. SEALs came from all over the United States and they could have met anywhere at any time. And then, there was also the motivation he had to consider. It would take a great deal of persuasion to make any of his brothers turn on the rest of the team.

There was Trace O'Reilly, whom he had known since they both joined the navy ten years ago. Trace had lost a brother to narcotics and was vehemently opposed to drug use. He was quite vocal about his desire to put an end to the drug trade.

Cameron Wilbanks came to them from a small town in the south, which meant he had strong morals, a faith background and took pride in being a hero. And though he was a terrific, intelligent guy, he didn't seem to have the street sophistication to get mixed up in the drug cartels. Cameron just didn't seem likely to get involved with anything the least bit illegal.

Loren McFarland hoped to become a full-time pastor and missionary when his stint with the SEALs was over, and though that didn't necessarily exclude him from any wrongdoing, Micah couldn't remember ever meeting a more caring, genuine guy. McFarland tried to keep them all on the right path every day.

Micah worked his way down through all sixteen members of his platoon, still coming up blank. He couldn't think of a single guy who had motive to carry out such reprehensible actions. Frank, Javier, Lucas, Jonathan, Abdullah, Carey, Dalton, Jeremiah, Sean and Yordi… They all seemed just as trustworthy as they had always been. They were a tight-knit group, so he felt sure he would be aware of it if any of the men had experienced a change in attitude. Dalton Taggert was the only one experiencing any sort of problems outside of navy life, and he seemed to be dealing with it just fine.

Micah's thoughts were interrupted when a slight scratching noise commanded his attention. It was quiet enough to be ignored by most, but Micah recognized it immediately. Someone was picking the lock on the care unit door.

He glanced at Keilani's sleeping form. He hated to wake her, but knew it was necessary, just in case there was more than one man. It could be just a distraction.

"Keilani, get up. We have company. Come with me. Hurry." He nudged her gently until she began to stir.

"Is it Gus?" She was struggling to get her eyes open, and clearly hadn't registered his comment about the intruder. She was getting to her feet anyway.

"No, someone is picking the lock. We need to surprise them. Let's go." He had his Sig in one hand and grasped her hand with the other.

She was instantly more alert. Good girl. "What's the plan?"

"Ambush. As soon as the door opens. I don't want to shoot, though. I'd rather just tackle him and get some answers. But stay out of the way in case I have to wing him." He watched her face for understanding, and when she got it, he put her in place and moved to his.

The scratching slowed and stopped. There was an

almost imperceptible click. They waited, holding their breaths, but the door didn't open. Keilani sent him a confused look, but he only shook his head and gestured for her to wait. The perp could be listening to ascertain what awaited inside.

Micah was about to decide the intruder had changed his mind for some reason when the door suddenly swung open. A figure swathed from head to toe in all black stepped in and Micah launched himself at the man with the full force of his body weight. The man went down and they wrestled on the floor, fighting for dominance. Micah was patient, just kept battling for the upper hand. He knew he was one of the strongest men in his platoon, and by far the smartest. He didn't become an officer by chance.

Desperation made his opponent strong, and he continued to fight hard against Micah's superior strength. Micah pinned him to the floor with a forearm, but the man managed to wriggle free. Micah rolled with him, pulling one arm away from the man's body at an unnatural angle. The man only grunted and broke loose. When finally Micah got the upper hand once more, the man pulled a blade.

Now that was fighting dirty.

Enraged, Micah grasped the man's blade hand and twisted hard until the knife fell from his fingers, accompanied by a sharp cry. He used a couple of other maneuvers that he wished Keilani didn't have to witness, and finally he had the man subdued.

Even though he wore a dark hood that covered most of his face, Micah couldn't miss the widening of the man's eyes. It was much like a feral beast caught in a trap, but then the man's expression changed and Micah braced himself. He stiffened, wondering what his foe planned now. Micah released one hand to pull off the man's hood, hoping to catch him off guard, but the man was ready.

He relaxed, causing Micah's grip to involuntarily loosen. He slumped, loosening every single muscle in his body as if going unconscious.

"What…?" Micah fought for a good grip, but in a flash, the man wriggled free, and the metallic click of a pin hitting the floor prefaced the thud of a grenade. It wasn't even a split second before Micah was on his feet.

"Get down!" The shout from Micah's lungs accompanied his dive across the room to Keilani.

The blast rocked them, and debris rained down on them. Micah had one hand over his head, but his body shielded Keilani from most of the shrapnel. He felt a sharp pain as a piece hit him hard in the shoulder. It seemed forever before the debris settled around them and Micah felt it was safe to release her.

When he did, he rose to find his fears were realized once again.

The man was gone.

TEN

Keilani was finally getting a sense that maybe Lieutenant Micah Kent was human after all.

She was doing her best to be as gentle as possible and she had managed to find a numbing agent safe for use on humans among the things stocked for treating the cetaceans, but each time Micah winced, she was reminded he did indeed feel pain.

"Odd to see you aren't actually superhuman." Keilani grinned at him as she carefully extracted another bit of shrapnel from his shoulder. It was a messy wound, ragged edges filled with random bits of metal of various sizes. She had clipped the ragged edges of his torn shirt fabric out of the way so she could see to work.

He sucked in a breath between his teeth. "It's like you're digging around with flaming matches back there."

"That's what happens when you use your body as a human shield." She plucked at another piece of metal, trying to be gentler.

"So you'd rather be digging this out of yourself?" His back tensed again. She didn't miss the ripple of his muscles beneath his shirt, though she tried hard to put it out of her mind.

"No. I mean… I guess what I mean is thank you." She stopped prodding at his ruptured skin for a moment and he turned to look into her eyes. The tender emotion there nearly sent her over the edge.

Why did he have to be so emotionally distant?

She reminded herself it didn't matter anyway. He was her boss. There was no way they could become romantically involved, even if he wasn't a confirmed lifelong bachelor. And besides, thanks to her mother, she had seen how loving someone could completely wreck a person's life. She never wanted to be anything like her mother.

Micah was shrugging off her thanks. "I'm a SEAL. It's what I do."

His response angered her. That wasn't a typical Micah response. He was trying to hide his emotions by being arrogant.

She waved the tweezers at him. "Would it kill you to just respond graciously with a 'you're welcome' or something normal? What is wrong with you?"

"Right now my left shoulder has a hole blown in it, you're digging shrapnel out of it with what feels like flaming knives, and I had our guy but lost him— again—because I just couldn't wait to see who he was and loosened my grip before he was secure. Is there anything I missed?" Micah practically growled at her as he finished.

"Yeah, you forgot about the mistreatment of the dolphins and the forty-eight-plus-hours you've gone without sleep." She wasn't about to let him off easy right now.

"I'm used to going without sleep. I'm a—"

"SEAL, yes, I know. As if you'd let me forget. But being a SEAL doesn't mean you have to be an iceberg."

He was staring her down, and she stared right back, unflinching.

Finally, he spoke in a terrifyingly quiet voice. "Yes, it does."

Keilani had no idea what to say to that. Did he really believe that?

He turned away from her once more and she hesitated for only a moment before resuming her vigil. His reaction stung nearly as much as she imagined his flesh did at the wound site right now. *This is why you shouldn't let your heart get involved with a man, especially this one.* It seemed he was too stubborn to even allow himself to feel.

Keilani continued to work in silence for what felt like hours. If Micah's rigid posture was any indication, his anger hadn't dissipated. The tension between them stretched endlessly.

At last, she was certain the wound had been cleared of all debris, and she leaned back to stretch her stiff muscles. "It's clear, but I'm going to need to disinfect it before I stitch you up. It's going to hurt."

His teeth ground together on his reply. "Why do I feel like that prospect doesn't bother you much right now?"

She fired right back at him. "Maybe because of the way you're acting."

"Maybe you're the reason I'm acting this way." His eyes narrowed, but emotion blazed in their depths.

"Don't try to blame this on me. You make your own choices, and a *SEAL* has been trained to have self-control, right?" She leaned toward him at the taunt, knowing it was a dangerous thing to do.

Instead of shouting back at her, he leaned in, too. He seemed to think better of it, though, and pulled away. She was infused with boldness at the knowledge that he had been thinking of kissing her. She leaned forward, not wanting to lose the opportunity. He met her halfway, their lips meeting gently. He seemed unsure at first that she was okay with this, but then his kiss began to soften into a gentle caress. She felt like melting. Wonder filled her that so much tenderness could flood her at a man's touch. She sighed against his mouth.

In a flash, lucidity won out and he jerked away. "What are we doing?"

His hand went to his hair and he turned away. Keilani touched her lips. What was she thinking, kissing him like that? She stared at the back of his dark head, marveling at the churning of emotions rolling through her. Tenderness, joy and the thrill of his desire for her were quickly replaced by sadness, regret and the assurance that she could never kiss him again. She wanted to laugh, cry and scream all at the same time.

He finally turned back to her. "I know you kissed me, but I was thinking it. You just reacted. I'm sure a gentleman would apologize. But I can't. I'm not sorry. So—" he gestured to the small table where her wound-debriding tools sat, along with the disinfectant "—let's get this wound cleaned and be done with it."

If her shock was evident on her face, he didn't react to it. He just presented his back to her once more, the crimson wound glaring and prominent on his left shoulder through the rip in his shirt.

She didn't say a word, just picked up the disinfectant and poured it generously on the wound.

For once Micah just let the scream tear from his lips. If this pileup of emotions he was feeling didn't find some release, there was no telling what other stupid things he might do. So he let the physical pain mingle with the emotional pain and released it in one fierce warrior cry. To his surprise Keilani didn't even flinch. He had told her the truth. He wasn't sorry he had kissed her.

She was beautiful, inside and out. If he was the type of man to want a home and family, she would be everything he could need in a woman. Brave and strong, smart and kind—he couldn't think of anything she was lacking. The irony of the whole thing didn't escape him.

"I'm going to stitch it up now, okay?" Her voice was small, like she regretted the fact that she had to continue to hurt him.

"Yeah. Just hurry. We need to see about Gus and check on the other dolphins." He knew his tone was harsh, but he couldn't help it.

He turned just enough to see her frown as she prepared the needle. Her aptitude for medicine was amazing, be it human or animal. A sudden thought occurred to him.

"Why didn't you become a physician instead of a veterinarian? You'd have been very good at it."

She held the needle aloft, looking at it, not at him. "Animals are much easier to deal with than humans. They don't hurt you near as much."

Ouch. He knew that comment was aimed directly at him.

"That's probably true, but you don't seem like the type to avoid challenge." He closed his eyes as her gloved hand touched his shoulder near the wound, bracing himself for the needle stick.

"Maybe not, but it seems pretty silly not to avoid pain any time it's possible. There is enough pain in life that we can't avoid." The sudden stick of the needle into his flesh only emphasized her words.

"I've always found that there are many times when the outcome is worth the pain. Sometimes you have to take the risk." His words came through gritted teeth as she worked the needle in and out of his shoulder.

She paused in her stitching. "Physical pain, you mean? I'm not sure emotional pain would fall into the same category."

He didn't comment, so she continued. "You agree, don't you? Why else would you still be single? You don't want to experience heartbreak any more than anyone else does."

"Oh, I definitely plan to remain single. It isn't that, though."

She furrowed her brow. "What do you mean?"

"Sometimes it's necessary for change. Growth." He breathed deeply, in and out.

"But?" She pulled the wound together more tightly with her free hand.

"But sometimes it's not. You should use common sense. Avoid it when it doesn't help anything. I've learned some pain isn't really worth the risk." He knew he sounded like a jerk, but he didn't know how else to make her understand.

"Maybe you've just never been in love." Her words were quiet and reverent. He thought they might even be a little bit hopeful, but maybe that was his own wishful thinking.

"Have you?" He looked over his shoulder at her.

The pain that crept across her face was an answer in itself. "I thought I might be. Once."

He waited a moment, still watching her, but she never elaborated. "What happened?"

The needle paused. "It didn't end well."

She was quiet a moment longer, then the needle started up again. "His name was Jackson Carrigan. I met him through a mutual friend. We became friends right away and eventually started dating. But I guess I didn't know him as well as I thought. We went out with friends one night. I'd been up most of the night before with a sick whale at the aquatic park where I worked at the time. He disappeared a time or two, leaving me with people I barely knew. Finally, I decided I just wanted him to take me home."

She paused to cut the thread and tie off the stitches, then leaned back, looking skyward as she continued. "It took me a while to find him. When I did, he was with another girl. It was…pretty obvious what they had been doing. I managed to get another ride home, but the next day he showed up at my door. When I told him I didn't want to see him again he grew very angry and demanded to know why. I told him I couldn't stomach a cheater and he grew angry and started yelling. I slammed the door on him."

"Did he leave you alone then?" Micah had a strong desire to find the man and break every bone in his body.

"Not for a while. He finally realized I meant what I said, but not before several loud arguments and a restraining order."

"Did he ever try to see you again?"

"Just once, but my grandfather intervened. I think that's why Jackson finally let it go."

"Well, I'm thankful for your grandfather, then. I guess that's when you learned to shoot?" She nodded. But the anger didn't leave his body. "You thought you were in love with the guy?"

"At first. He was very sweet and attentive in the beginning. I mean, I guess I never saw him angry before that, so I suppose I just thought he was easygoing and kind. He opened doors for me, spoke politely to my grandparents and brought me extravagant gifts. I just couldn't help thinking he was this wonderful gentleman. But I fell in love with a facade. It wasn't real." Her expression was faraway and melancholy. Micah's anger intensified.

"I'd be glad to teach him a lesson for you." His tone was cheerful.

When she blinked wide-eyed at him for a moment, he thought he might have taken his teasing too far. Then she laughed. "That's good to know."

He cracked his knuckles for emphasis, grinning. "Want me to?"

She laughed again, and he found he wanted to keep hearing it. "No, that's okay. I'm trying to forgive and forget. He will receive what he deserves."

He made a dejected face at her in hopes of getting another laugh, but she just smiled. He wasn't exactly disappointed with that, though.

Her smile made him forget all about what he was looking for anyway.

ELEVEN

Keilani knew she should let it go and just allow Micah some breathing room, but she couldn't be sure he would ever choose to open up to her on his own. Pushing the issue wasn't usually something she did in matters like this, so it took a few tries to figure out how to ask him.

"You changed the subject again without answering me. But I was wrong, wasn't I? You have been in love. That's why you don't want to risk it. Someone hurt you and you don't want to go through that again." Keilani finished sterilizing the tools she had been using on his wound and put them away.

He was staring into space. "I thought I was once. I was wrong."

She wasn't about to let it go that easily. "How were you wrong?"

"It wasn't love. She betrayed me." He still didn't look at her, but he did continue this time. "Her name was Jade. We pretty much grew up together and when we were teenagers, we fell in love. Or so I thought. We were together through most of high school and when the time came to go to college, she just assumed I would go where she wanted to go. She had high aspirations. She wanted to be an architect. When I decided to enlist in the navy instead of following her to the university she was upset, but after much discussion we eventually decided to make it work anyway."

He stopped, looking into Keilani's eyes for a long moment. She nodded her encouragement and he finally continued.

"We made it until Christmas. But while she was home on break, she called me crying. She wanted me to come home. I told her she was being ridiculous. She knew I couldn't just quit and leave. I couldn't talk any sense into her, though, and the next day I got a call from a really good friend named Jordan. He had gone to the same university as Jade and planned to be a lawyer. He told me he was in love with Jade and that they had been seeing each other for a few weeks. She never admitted it to me herself. I knew Jordan was telling me the truth, so I broke up with her. I knew I'd done the right thing when they got married a few months later. She was pregnant, and far enough along to prove what Jordan had told me."

Keilani was devastated for him. "Wow, that must have been really terrible."

He shrugged the shoulder that wasn't injured. "It happens."

"That doesn't mean it's easy to get over. Do you still care for her?"

"It was a long time ago." He tried to leave it at that.

"Still, if you loved her the feelings could linger—"

"Like I said, I just thought I loved her." He turned away.

He obviously wasn't going to tell her what she wanted to know. It frustrated her. She wanted to help him, but he clearly wasn't willing to trust her with his feelings. Maybe he never would.

The past several hours had been long and tiring, and Keilani found she was feeling discouraged. She didn't like the self-pity that tried to creep in on her, so she busied herself with checking on the dolphins and reorganizing supplies. If Micah noticed, he chose to give her some space.

Things were quiet for a long time, which just made it more difficult for Keilani to work off the funk she was in. The events of the past couple of days had really begun to wear on her. Finally, she slumped into a chair in the corner and just let the tears fall. She didn't want to disappoint Micah by showing weakness, but she couldn't find the strength to hold it together anymore. She couldn't take it.

He surprised her by crouching beside her in concern, brows knit together as he grasped her hand. "Hey, I'm sorry. I should have made sure you were okay earlier. At least helped you keep your mind off things. I'm not good at this stuff. What can I do to help?"

She shook her head, tears falling faster in the face of his concern. "There's nothing. I'm sorry. I'm trying—"

He cut her off with a wave of his hand. "Nothing to be sorry for. You've done great. You must be exhausted, and between the attacker and the dolphins, you've not had a chance to breathe. If you can just hold on a little longer, I think we are about to catch this guy."

This comment got her attention. "Really? Why do you say that?"

He was looking at his phone. "I just got a message from my CO, Captain Jarvis, saying he was checking into a strong lead here on base. It may not pan out, but even if it doesn't, I have a feeling it will lead us in the right direction."

"You're sure? I feel like we've had a lot of near misses so far." She wiped at the corner of one eye.

"Yes, I'm sure. Don't get discouraged. I promise I'll keep you safe. For as long as it takes." He squeezed her hand.

Her thoughts went to what would happen next. If they did finally catch this guy, how would things change between her and Micah? Would he still want to work with her? He might not have a choice, but it would be difficult if he wanted her to leave. And how would they ever keep things professional after being so close throughout these past few days? And then there was that kiss…

She had to put it out of her mind. They would just have to deal with things as they came. Nothing would be changed by her worry.

"You okay?" Micah was gazing at her with pronounced intensity as if willing his own strength into her.

"Yes. I mean, I will be." She stood and took a deep breath. "I have an idea about how we can help."

His expression became guarded. "Oh, yeah? How's that?"

"What if we send in a team to clear out their little work area? Could we attract their attention and force them into action so we could catch them and end this?" She was done with this. She would rather endanger herself than keep living in constant fear. She was grasping, surely, but she wanted to feel useful somehow.

"The navy will take care of it when Captain Jarvis gives the order. I'm sorry things aren't moving more quickly." His tone said he didn't like where this was going.

Keilani didn't care. She had to convince him. She

was desperate to get this over with. "They're after me, right? So what if I act as bait, of a sort. We can make it look like you had to leave me alone with the dolphins without you. That would make it seem like I would be an easier target. They might think it's easier to come after us one at a time. The team moves in to take out their little operation when they come after me. You could have a couple of guys situated to take them down once their underwater base is secured."

"That's putting you in too much danger. Who knows how long it could take to secure it, and the main reason they are after you is to kill you. That wouldn't take these guys long at all. And there is always the chance they could turn around and try to use you as bait to get to me." He was being blunt and showed no remorse for it.

She felt a little uneasy about the thought of them using her to try to get to Micah, even though she didn't think it would work. He would protect the dolphins first.

She pushed the thought aside. "I'm sure you can handle whatever they throw at you. And what if I give them some incentive to keep me alive?" She thrust her chin out at him.

"Like what?" His thunderous expression said he couldn't think of a single reason he might like.

"Maybe we take something of theirs—or at least something they perceive to be theirs. We could use something valuable such as one of the dolphins they are using. We could hide it somewhere safe and then when we claim to know where it is, they might be willing to keep me alive a little longer."

He shook his head. "Or they might just torture you until you tell. It's too risky. We'll have to find another way."

She was running out of ammo. Why did he have to be so stubborn?

"Lieutenant Kent." A deep voice from the door startled Keilani. They turned to see the same officer from earlier.

Micah faced him, no surprise on his face. If he hadn't known the man was there, no one would have ever guessed by his reaction. "What is it, Petty Officer Taggert?"

"Just received a call from Petty Officer Carraway. It's not good news." The man's face was a steel mask.

"What news?" Micah's tone bordered on impatient.

"Petty Officer Emmett McCauley has been shot. He's still alive, but he's in critical condition."

The game had just changed.

Micah concentrated on breathing in and out until his anger numbed enough to prevent him from doing anything too rash. Keilani's idea suddenly held far more appeal. Their enemy was obviously trying to draw them out, but Micah was done playing games. He was going to end this.

"How did it happen?" He made the mistake of glancing in Keilani's direction and her crumpled expression lit the fuse on his anger once again.

"McCauley was leaving your house. It looks like someone was waiting for him." The damage done to the house by the Molotov cocktail had been minimal but Emmett had been there trying to clean up the inside.

Even though Taggert was as rigid as any naval officer should be, there was clear regret in his eyes as he explained what happened. Everyone liked Emmett.

"So he was specifically targeted." He could almost hear his own teeth grinding together.

"It would appear so."

Micah dismissed Taggert and the man fled. Micah realized his anger must be more apparent than he thought.

Keilani wasn't intimidated by his obvious wrath, however. "So are you ready to consider my plan?"

He didn't answer her immediately and she started to speak again. "I'm sorry. I feel like—"

"Don't even think about saying it's your fault. We're all expendable to these guys now that we've seen the evidence of their operation." He began walking around the room, picking things up and moving them, knowing she was wondering why.

"I— Okay. What are you doing?" She cocked her head to one side.

"Reordering things."

"Reordering…things? What? Why?"

"It helps me focus. I can't just stare into space and come up with a solution. Especially not when I'm angry." He didn't look at her, just kept moving around the room.

He could feel her staring at him and finally stopped. "It's a trick I had to learn a long time ago. When I first entered SEAL training I had real problems trying to focus. I worked through it, but before I was recommended to take over the job with the dolphins it became much worse."

"How?" Keilani's brow wrinkled.

"It's hard to explain. I told you I had what my superiors thought was a natural gift with the cetaceans. What I didn't tell you was that it actually saved my career. I was dangerously close to being asked to leave the program, even though I made it through the training and selection process."

Keilani's eyes widened. "What happened?"

"It was a training exercise, but I didn't know it at the time. I made a mistake—a big one—which could have cost many of my team members their lives, all because of my lack of focus. I got angry and lost it. I was put on probation and sent to a naval psychologist. He told me I had to learn to focus and control my anger or I would never survive in the navy. He quickly determined that I was dealing with some ADHD issues. I had two choices. I could either medicate and be considered useless by the navy, or I could learn some coping skills that would help me in every aspect of my life." He started moving around the room again.

"So you started reordering things." She sounded a little awed by it.

"That was one of the methods. We came up with several options along the way. That wasn't enough for the navy, of course. When I was recommended for the job with the dolphins, my CO still hesitated. They gave a couple of other guys a shot at it, but the dolphins were the ones who really got me the job. They didn't take to anyone else the way they did to me. It was almost like they knew we needed each other."

"They have some of the most well-developed brains of any mammals. They chose you." Her soft tone confirmed that she realized he was thinking it, even if he didn't want to admit it.

"Well, I'm grateful they did. I would have never survived my enlistment if they had sent me back to being a sailor." Telling the story had calmed his anger somewhat, but he still felt an urgent need to come up with a solution.

"We're going to get these guys, Micah." Her calm statement stilled him once more. Something about the collected way she addressed him soothed what was left of his anger.

Before Micah could respond, however, Xavier burst through the door. "You've gotta get her out of here, man. These guys are through playing around."

Micah was thrown even more off balance by the normally calm Xavier running in like that. He had never seen his friend so rattled.

Micah was asking questions before Xavier could catch his breath. "What else has happened?"

"They've found Emmett's shooter. He's a former SEAL. Remember the guy you were asking me about? Jarnigan?"

Micah nodded. "It was him?"

"Yeah, but the only reason they found him is because he's dead. His body was discovered in a dumpster in the sketchy part of town. Someone is getting rid of evidence. But that's not all."

Micah felt his face harden into a stone mask.

Xavier pulled out a piece of paper and handed it to Micah. It was a neatly drawn map of the base, highlighting the dolphin enclosures and the veterinary facilities, which were marked with bold red Xs. The top of the note had a cryptic message. "You mess with my operation, I mess with yours." The bottom of the note had the single word BOOM! spelled out in large letters.

"Apparently, this guy thinks he's cute." Micah was through being intimidated. "It could be just an empty threat."

Xavier silently began pushing buttons on his phone. He handed it to Micah, who took it reluctantly. "They've already found two."

Micah examined the picture and let out a low whistle. "These are professional." Then he turned to Keilani. "We're getting you out of here, just in case."

"But what about the dolphins?" Keilani shook her head at him as if she wouldn't leave without them.

"They should be relatively safe from any explosives under the water." Micah started nudging her out.

"Relatively?" She didn't look convinced.

He frowned at her. "I can't make absolute guarantees. But your safety is more important. We have to get you out."

She glared at him for a moment, but finally started moving toward the door. "What about the dolphins' safety? They're important to me."

"We'll turn them out into the pens farthest from the center of the base, closer to the ocean. They're smart, remember? They can identify bombs." He motioned for her to move faster.

"But do they know to stay away from them? Do they understand what bombs do?" She wasn't easily persuaded. Her mental state seemed to be growing more fragile.

He fixed her with a serious stare. "Of course they do. They are trained to find them. And I just explained to you how much these guys mean to me. Do you really think I would just abandon them if they were in any real danger?" Micah looked her in the eye until she shook her head.

"No. I'm sure you wouldn't." She glanced at Xavier, who was waiting to follow them out.

Micah watched Keilani's skin go white before she

began to hurry out. He knew of only one safe place to take her right now. He would have to contact his CO and let him know, but first he needed her off the base, and maybe even off this side of the bay. They would have to go to a safe house, but the only secure way to get to one was by helicopter. He had a feeling their vehicles might also be loaded with explosives. The bomb threat was most likely a maneuver to flush them out, so their adversaries were definitely going to be pulling out all the stops at this point.

Micah was on the radio in an instant. The base was being cleared while the bomb squad went to work, so the request for helicopter transport might take a little longer than usual. In the interim, he would take every precaution to keep Keilani out of harm's way.

"We're going to have to go back and release Gus into a safer tank. He's too exposed in the ICU. By that time we can head out to meet the helicopter." He gathered up everything he could carry in the way of weapons and handed Keilani a Kevlar vest and helmet he had pulled from a storage closet. "Put these on."

"Are you sure? I'm not certain Gus is ready to be released." She was turning the vest over and over as she questioned him, clearly not sure about which end was which.

He reached over and helped her put it on. It wasn't that difficult, so he knew she was flustered. "He'll be better off released than taking his chances with the explosives. He's not had the exposure to the bomb detection procedures that most of the other dolphins have."

Keilani fastened the vest and put on the helmet while Micah and Xavier did the same with theirs. He slid Gus out into the tank with little fuss and watched him swim slowly into the next one. Eventually, he swam away from the base to join some of the other dolphins, who circled him a time or two before forming a protective shield around him.

Micah put Keilani's Glock in her hand. "When in doubt, shoot first. Let's go."

They burst through the door to the outside, the California sunshine blindingly bright in their faces. Micah didn't need time to adjust, just grabbed Keilani by the hand without hesitation, almost dragging her along with him. The helicopter was landing a few dozen yards away and he rushed her in its direction.

The wind from the propeller blades threw her off balance as they hurried closer, and he took valuable seconds to steady her before urging her along. Xavier rushed ahead to help her climb inside, and then he shut the door behind Micah as he waved goodbye to them.

"Xavier isn't coming?" Keilani shouted her question.

Micah shook his head. "He has to stay and help defuse any bombs they find."

She paled once again at the reminder. "What if they don't find them all in time?"

She was probably blaming herself again. "They will. They're experts."

The confidence in his tone seemed to calm her somewhat. She allowed the copilot to instruct her on strapping in properly and sat back and closed her eyes. Micah uttered a silent prayer, not only for her safety, but also for her emotional well-being.

This life wasn't for everyone. In fact, it wasn't for many people at all. Which was why he had to remind himself to remain diligent on his vow to remain single, even though Keilani challenged it at every turn.

TWELVE

Keilani swallowed back the nervous energy that swept through her as the helicopter began to rise into the air. She had never flown in a helicopter before, but she found the experience amazing, even preoccupied as she was with the current situation. She could feel Micah watching her, but she chose to ignore him for a little longer while she took in the new experience.

The landscape grew smaller as the chopper dipped and swayed, giving her stomach a hard nudge here and there. She felt exhilarated and a little anxious all at once. There was a lot of air between herself and the ground, and unlike in an airplane, she felt small and vulnerable—but somehow free at the same time.

Before she could even get settled in, they were landing. A twinge of disappointment flickered and swelled in her chest. The runners were nearing the ground and she took a deep breath that ended on a sigh. "I've never flown in a helicopter before. I know you're wondering."

A sideways grin brought out one dimple in his cheek. "Guilty. Trying to let you process." He helped her from the helicopter as soon as the rotors slowed enough to keep them stable on the ground.

"Funny, that's what I've been doing." She smiled in return.

"You seem to be handling it well." He let his grin fade, a serious look penetrating her defenses.

"The flight or the bomb threat?" Keilani had both on her mind, despite the distracting thoughts she had when he looked at her that way. He was guiding her toward the safe house, a small but neat little home in a secluded cul-de-sac. The neighborhood was quiet. There were fences around all of the homes, and the one they were approaching looked like just another family residence.

"Both, actually. I know you're still worried about Gus—about all the dolphins." His eyes were piercing, demanding honesty from her. She tried to keep moving, but she came near to stumbling over nothing at all.

"Yes, but I trust you. If you believe they will be safe, then I do, too." She looked at the ground, hoping she hadn't said too much. But before she did, she caught a glimpse of his reaction. If she wasn't mistaken, there was a hint of panic mingled with pleasure at her words.

"You're very dedicated to your work." His statement was so vague, her eyes returned to him in surprise. It was so far removed from the reaction she had anticipated. He was unlocking the door to the brick cottage.

"To tell you the truth, I almost gave up working with dolphins in the beginning." The comment was out before she could stop it. She took in the cozy living room without really seeing what was there. Micah followed her in and wasted no time in closing the door.

"What do you mean? I can't imagine you doing anything else." He moved to the thermostat on the wall and adjusted the switches to "On" before returning his attention to her.

Cool air flowed from the vent and Keilani realized she had opened up something, as well. His curiosity was piqued and now he wouldn't let it go. She would have to let the story flow out also. "Well, I'm honestly a bit envious of the ease with which the dolphins took to you. My experience was much different."

He sat down across from her on a cream-colored sofa and gave her his full attention. "How so?"

She felt heat creeping into her cheeks. "They didn't like me at first. Didn't respect me, I guess I should say. They tried to bully me and intimidate me. It sounds silly to you, I'm sure."

He shook his head. "Not at all. They can be willful creatures. Probably sensed some hesitation on your part."

"Exactly. I had never spent much time around animals that large when I began working with them and I was afraid of embarrassing myself. The job was supposed to help me get through vet school. But I didn't realize how quickly they would pick up on my inexperience. When I attempted to give them a command, they would do the direct opposite. Sometimes they would ignore me completely. They had me in tears by the end of the second day. I was having a tiny bit of success with one of the younger dolphins when Flintstone, one of the orneriest of the bunch, came along and knocked over the bucket of fish I was using as a reward. The other dolphins swarmed, knocking me out of the way, and of course, I lost all progress with the young dolphin."

"I'm sure you were ready to quit at that point. How did you win them over?" He watched her smooth her hand over a sofa pillow while she gathered the words to continue.

"I didn't have a choice really, and to be honest, they

actually won me over in the end. Flintstone ended up being my favorite. I just kept trying. One day my boss told me I was going to have to act like one would with any group of wild animals—be the alpha. For some reason that clicked with me. I had been trying to be one of them instead of becoming their leader.

"Flintstone was the hardest case, but I gained his respect one day when I caught another handler being unnecessarily rough with him. I put a stop to it right then, and she was fired not too long after. Who knows how long she had been abusing them. Flintstone seemed to realize what I had done for them all, and he became fiercely loyal to me after that—to the point that he embarrassed a new kid when he thought the guy was being rude to me one day." She tried to blink the tears away, but she felt them pricking at the corners of her eyes.

Micah noticed. "Did something else happen with Flintstone?"

She nodded. "He died. Just before I left, he got a terrible infection. He was sick for about a week and then one morning he just…died. I felt like I should have done more for him."

"Is that why you decided to focus on marine mammals?"

"Yes. I promised Flintstone I would do something to honor his memory and make things better for captive cetaceans." She smiled. "I'm not sure how I'm doing so far, though. And time may run out."

"Not even for a second do I want to hear you talk like that. And you're doing fantastic." He jumped up from the sofa. The curtains were tightly closed, but a sliver of light fell across his face, making his gray eyes seem to glow. "Let's see if we can come up with some food.

Xavier is supposed to check in with me as soon as he can. Until then I need a distraction."

There wasn't much in the way of preparation for a real meal, but some nonperishable items had been stocked for such an occasion. Microwave popcorn, bottled water and some canned fruit provided an adequate snack, so they enjoyed a quick picnic in the living room at the coffee table while Micah searched out a movie Keilani might be interested in watching from the long list on the TV.

Keilani was impressed by the accommodations, including Wi-Fi and all the latest streaming subscriptions. "How often is this place used?"

He sent her a rueful glance. "Far more often than anyone would like."

"Obviously. I guess it must be if the utilities and the Wi-Fi stay on all the time." She looked around the clean, comfortable sitting area and adjoining kitchen.

"It's used for a couple of other things here and there, but I can't tell you what. We can only hope our guy on the inside doesn't think about it." He winked at her over a handful of buttery popcorn.

"Top-secret SEAL stuff?" She took a swig of water.

"Something like that."

"Is it ever difficult not to tell what you know? Like, have you ever almost slipped up and told something you shouldn't?" She pondered a spoonful of peaches.

He thought for a moment. "I suppose I probably have, early on. But you get into the habit of being tight-lipped. You have to always consider your words very carefully when you're a SEAL. Saying the wrong thing can easily get people killed."

"Ouch." She swallowed. "I guess that would be a pretty big deterrent."

"It is, but it makes you realize, no matter the situation, our words always have the power to affect someone else's life."

"I never really considered that, but you're right." She set down the spoon. "Our actions, too. I'm finding that out."

"You didn't do anything wrong, Keilani. Don't assume you did, just because you were the one to discover the smugglers' operational location."

"If I hadn't seen them that morning, I wouldn't have placed the dolphins—and us—in all this danger. Going for a swim that morning was a terrible idea."

"The dolphins were already in danger. If anyone should feel guilt, it's me because they were using my dolphins as drug mules right under my nose." He turned away.

"You were working on it. You couldn't have known." Keilani got up and moved toward him. The urge to put a hand on his arm in comfort was difficult to ignore.

"I should have." His steel jaw was clenched tight.

"How?" She let her reserve go and rested a hand on his arm.

He looked at her hand for a moment. "I don't know. I just should have figured it out. I should have been more attentive to everything that was going on."

Keilani pulled in a breath and held it for a moment. She had to tell him. He wasn't going to like it.

"Micah, I have a confession to make." She bit her lip, waiting.

His eyes darkened and she had the terrible suspicion

that he had received bad news in such a way at some point in the past. "What do you mean?"

She stared into his eyes, hoping for understanding. "When I first came to work with you, I was asked by someone in the World Animal Protection Agency to report back to them on the welfare of navy marine mammals. I haven't done so because I don't believe the navy is at fault. But they are going to want to know."

His face hardened. "And what do you plan to tell them?"

"That the situation was out of your control and has been rectified." Keilani reached out to him.

He pulled back. "So you're going to report that the navy has been lax enough to let their dolphins be used as drug mules?"

Keilani shrugged. "No, I don't think I can do that if I want to keep my job. But eventually they will find out the truth. Then it will look like a cover-up. What would you have me tell them?"

"Nothing at all. They have never been anything but a problem for our program. I'd rather they mind their own business." He ran a hand through his hair. "Why didn't you tell me?"

Keilani looked at her toes. "I didn't think you would understand."

"You were right about that much. And I was right not to trust you." His face hardened and he turned away, his stiff posture a testament to his anger.

"Micah, please. I thought I was doing the right thing. The welfare of these animals is important to me." She hated the pleading tone in her voice, but she couldn't prevent it.

"And it's also important to me. You should have told

me we were being investigated." His voice was cold, unfeeling.

"I know that now. I didn't know you at first. Didn't know any of you. And really, it isn't an investigation. They just wanted to know if there should be one." Keilani let all of her emotions show through her eyes, pleading with him to understand.

He ignored it. "As soon as you're safe, I want you to leave. I'm going to request that the admiral dismiss you. He can find someone else or not. I don't care. He won't take your deception well, either."

"For what it's worth, I'm sorry I didn't tell you." She tried again, but his response was just coldness.

His phone chose that moment to demand his attention. "It's Xavier."

He picked it up and left the room.

Would he ever forgive her? She had wondered all along if she should tell him. Now this rift seemed irreparable. He was taking it much worse than she had expected, and, knowing his history with the dolphins, she could understand why.

Keilani watched him go, her heart aching for him. They were a fine pair, she realized, each blaming themselves for the misdeeds of others.

She wandered into the kitchen, cleaning up the dishes they had used for the canned fruit and throwing away their trash. On a whim, she decided to make coffee. It was likely they would have a long afternoon ahead of them.

She could hear the steady cadence of Micah's rich voice as it rose and fell in conversation. She couldn't make out what he was saying, but the steady strength of his voice reassured her in a way she couldn't define. He made her long for something she had no right to—a home and a family with him. No matter how she told herself it would never happen, she couldn't stop longing for it. A picture formed in her mind before she could stop it—a dark-haired little girl with Keilani's high cheekbones and Micah's deep gray eyes.

She pushed the image aside, frustrated with herself for letting the thoughts invade her psyche. She should have better control over her thoughts. Her chest ached from his recent rejection and she fought the urge to give in to tears.

Taking mugs from the cabinet, she made two black coffees, then added a touch of cream and two spoonfuls of sugar to one of them. She wouldn't ask herself how she knew exactly how Micah liked his coffee after only a few short days. It was ridiculous how much attention she had paid the man. She really did know better.

His footsteps rounded the corner and her heart picked up speed. Funny how his mere presence made her thrilled to see him, even knowing he was angry with her. He had such an automatic effect on her.

"They believe they have located and defused all the bombs. One went off before they could get to it, but no one was hurt. It was in an empty section of offices that had already been cleared. Easily repaired."

Keilani sighed. "That's a relief. So we can go back now?"

His expression turned into a frown. "No. I want to keep you here until these men are caught. I'm sorry if you had other plans."

"Oh. No. I mean, that is, I just wanted to check on Gus. And Emmett."

"Emmett is recovering. Xavier promised to keep an

eye out for Gus. It's my job to keep you safe." He strode closer now, strong and powerful, his presence almost overwhelming. Her heart rate jumped and pounded.

She swallowed. "I'm safe."

"Permanently." He said it firmly, and though she knew what he meant, it created a picture in her mind of white dresses and forever. She had to stop this. It was more impossible now than ever, but that knowledge only seemed to make her long for it more than before.

"So we hide here? For how long?" She tried to inject a bite into her tone, but it fell short of the effect she wanted.

"As long as it takes."

He had his game face on again, and though Keilani wished she could be intimidated by it, she actually found it alarmingly attractive. She knew he wouldn't hurt her, but she pitied anyone else who tried. It made her feel safe and kind of special.

"How—how do they know they found all of the bombs? How many were there?" She wanted to distract herself from her thoughts almost as much as she wanted to know the answers.

He pressed his lips together and she felt sure he was trying to decide how much to tell her. "They used the map Xavier had. It was surprisingly accurate. Someone was trying to prove a point."

She focused on his words. "And?"

"There were twelve."

Her jaw should have hit the floor it dropped so low. "Twelve bombs? That could have blown the whole base sky high."

"But whoever this guy is, he gave them enough time

to defuse them all. Why? That's what I can't quite figure out." Micah began to pace.

"Does he get some kind of thrill from this?" Keilani was shaking her head.

"Maybe. But there's more to it than that."

"So he didn't really want to blow up the base. He knew how long they would need to locate and defuse all the bombs. He probably knew we would run. Why?" Keilani ticked off each point on a different finger.

Micah struck the heel of his hand to his head. "The dolphins. Of course. Maybe they wanted to isolate the dolphins. Or just get us away from them."

"What do you mean?" A cold chill was already snaking its way up her spine as Keilani asked.

"They've been using our dolphins, and they know we are on to them. They needed everyone out of the way so they could recover their drugs. They knew the base would be evacuated, but they had to make it real enough to keep everyone out long enough to take care of business." Micah looked horrified.

"You don't think…" Keilani couldn't quite say the words. It would be horrible if they hurt the dolphins. But if they killed them… How would Micah ever get over the loss?

He was dialing before she could finish speaking. "Xavier, the dolphins! I don't know what these guys are planning, but it has something to do with my dolphins. You have to go and keep an eye on them. Don't let them out of your sight."

Keilani hadn't realized Micah had Xavier on speakerphone until his voice rang ominously into the silence. "I was just about to call you. I came in to check on them for you and—bro, the dolphins are gone. Every last one."

THIRTEEN

The panic rushing through Micah was unlike any feeling he had ever known. He wanted to lash out in every way physically possible to relieve the feeling welling inside him. First Keilani's deception, which had cut far deeper than he wanted to admit, and now this.

"How?" He knew he screamed the word, but it was unavoidable. "Find them! How? We are on our way."

Turmoil. That was what this was. It was the only way to describe what he was feeling. This was a trap. He knew they probably had a solid plan to not only get their drugs from the dolphins, but also draw him and Keilani out so they could finally finish them off. But he also knew there was no way he could sit here and let someone else attempt to find his dolphins without doing everything he could to help. If he took Keilani with him, he played right into their hands. If he left her, she would be vulnerable. And if she was who he thought she was, there was no way she would sit on her hands while he looked for the missing dolphins. There was no easy solution.

In fact, Keilani had already sprung into action. "How

long before you can get us out of here? Do we have to take a helicopter back, too? How long will it take?"

He supposed it was his fault. He had told Xavier they were on their way. He shouldn't even want her near him at this point, but his heart didn't seem to be listening to his brain. He didn't want to leave her here, no matter how angry he was with her. And he was pretty angry at the moment. But he would still make sure she was absolutely safe.

And her expression—it brooked no argument.

He knew exactly how she felt.

By the time they got back, Xavier had done everything Micah had already thought of doing.

"The gates were all opened. Every single dolphin has been released into open waters. I don't have access to their tracking devices. How do you find them?" Xavier gestured around the empty enclosures.

"That's assuming their tracking devices haven't been disabled. Those dolphins have been in captivity for all or most of their lives. They aren't accustomed to being without a handler nearby in open waters. I have no idea how they will react." Micah was pacing again.

"We have to find them ASAP." Keilani stood, hands on hips, glaring at them both.

Before either man could respond, bullets ricocheted all around them from the open side of the dolphin bay. Someone would have to be shooting from somewhere offshore—in a boat, perhaps. Micah scanned the water, looking for a clue as they took cover.

"There's more than one shooter," Micah informed Keilani. "Keep close to me, but stay as low as possible."

She did as he asked and they belly-crawled their

way behind one of the partition walls near the entrance. While they were crawling, Micah noted where each shooter was. One in the northwest corner of the bay on a fishing boat, one to the east just beyond a civilian dock that ran on the outskirts of the facility, and a third shooter off to their left, his upper body hovering just above water where he crouched in one of the enclosure pens.

Micah began to rattle off code words to Xavier to see if he noticed the same details, keeping their voices low so the shooters wouldn't hear. He knew the main guy had to be someone on the inside. No one else knew everything the smugglers seemed to know. Keeping one eye on Keilani, he aimed his Sig at one of the shooters. He gave Xavier the signal.

Both men fired at the same time, taking out two of the shooters at once. The third man realized what had happened and fled.

"Come on." Micah motioned to Keilani. "Let's go find our dolphins."

Xavier nodded and gestured them forward. "Go ahead. I've got your six."

Micah led Keilani to a boat often used by the marine mammal program for the transport of cetaceans. He had no idea how they were going to round up dozens of AWOL navy dolphins, but he had to do something. The odds were that he would find them all sticking pretty close together, but where? The thought of even one of his dolphins being set upon by predators sent his blood pressure skyrocketing. The only thing he could do was go out and call to them using the commands he had taught them. Whether or not those would be effective in open waters so close to home was anybody's guess.

This was a different situation from any mission they'd encountered, and some of those dolphins had never even been out on an open water mission before.

Keilani looked every bit as distraught as he felt. He would have loved to comfort her, but he had no idea how. Guiding the boat through the surf and into the ocean, he kept both eyes on the horizon for any sign of his cetaceans. Those were his babies out there somewhere. He would never let them go without a fight.

His frustration intensified the farther they got from shore. Surely, there should be some sign of the dolphins by now. They couldn't have been out here that long. Waves rippled placidly in the distance. There was nothing to catch his eye.

Keeping the boat on a steady path, Micah held to the course. *Think like a dolphin*, he commanded himself. *If you'd been in that enclosure your whole life, where would you go?*

Nothing came to him. They would just be happy to be free, right? Go exploring, swim unencumbered, dive and leap… And go see new sights, of course. The reef. They would head for the reef. It would be a marine mammal's playground.

Micah turned the boat in the direction of the reef. Keilani gave him a questioning look.

"The reef," he explained. "They've probably gone to the reef."

She nodded, but his attention was drawn to a low whine in the distance. A glance over his shoulder confirmed his fears. They were being followed.

It was a speedboat, and making better time than they were, so it was gaining on them quickly. The transport boat was maxed out. The speedboat came within range and began to fire on them. Keilani hunched below the bow as Micah tried to maneuver away from their pursuer. There wasn't much he could do to evade the faster boat. It had all been part of an elaborate trap. Deliver a bomb threat. Isolate the dolphins. Retrieve their drugs and then release the dolphins so Micah and Keilani would go out looking for them alone. And now the men would apprehend them in a much faster boat. He was going to have to think fast.

"Drive." Handing the wheel over to Keilani, Micah began to fire back, but with little success.

He was pondering whether they should jump ship or just wait on their pursuer to catch up when a bullet struck the propeller of the transport boat. It began to sputter, just as another sound registered. The gurgling could only mean their boat was taking on water. They were about to sink. Keilani cried out, but he had to keep focused.

Micah tried to keep firing, but the man in the speedboat was upon them, and he winged Micah in the shooting arm just before drawing up beside them.

"Sorry, brother, but I'm going to have to take this woman off your hands." A familiar voice spoke from behind a mask just before a fist connected with his jaw and everything went black.

Keilani had never hyperventilated before, but she was about to now.

She struggled with all her might, biting, kicking and screaming as the man dragged her into the speedboat. The sight of Micah's invincible form slumped over in the sinking transport boat as they sped away was burned indelibly into her memory. How would she ever live with herself if she got out of this alive and he didn't?

The driver of the speedboat tied her securely before tossing her into a seat and heading back toward shore. The zip ties were biting into her wrists with fervor, but all she could think about was Micah, unconscious and sinking slowly with the transport boat. Helplessness overtook her and she closed her eyes. All the little moments she had spent with Micah over the past few days ran together, and she felt the loss deep down. She knew he hadn't wanted a relationship, a commitment, or any type of future with her, but she didn't want him to die not knowing that she cared about him. No, it was much more than just caring. She loved him. Like it or not, she had fallen for him. At this moment it really didn't matter to her whether he returned her affection or not; she simply wanted him to know he was loved.

Waves rocked the speedboat, driving the nose up into the air and then crashing back down, but Keilani barely noticed any of it. Tears blurred her vision while her chest nearly exploded with the pain. Micah's gray eyes dancing over his steel-jawed frown filled her thoughts, along with images of Micah playing with the dolphins like a child with a new puppy and doing the hard work of helping her secure the injured Gus and Rhianna when they needed treatment. They had shared so many things in a very short time. And they'd worked so well together, as if they had been doing it for years.

Keilani's musings were interrupted when the waves began hitting the boat at a different angle. Her abductor had turned the boat away from shore and was heading parallel to the coastline away from the base. What was that about? He must have wanted to trick Micah into believing that was where they were going just in case he managed to survive and awakened before they were out of sight. The farther they went from the base, the more her hopes of any rescue dissipated. No one would know to look for her way out here, even if anyone realized she was missing. It was completely up to her to escape and somehow get back to Micah.

Her mind spun with a desperation she had never known, trying to discern any way it might be possible to get the upper hand. She needed to get back to Micah in time to rescue him, but looking at the burly man who had taken her, she knew she couldn't possibly overpower him. The only hope she might have would be in outsmarting him somehow. The question remaining was how.

She studied him carefully, looking for anything that might indicate a weakness of any kind. What about this man might she use to get an advantage? He wore a wetsuit and a mask, not uncommon for a diver in the cold waters of the Pacific, and the neoprene only emphasized his strength. He moved athletically and didn't seem to have any type of physical impairments. Of course he didn't, if he was a SEAL like Micah suspected. The man had his attention focused between driving the boat and looking at a cell phone he had anchored to the dash. Was he using some type of GPS to guide him to their destination?

Just great. If he didn't even know how to get there, how would anyone ever find them? It just reinforced her theory that she would have to outmaneuver this guy on her own and very soon, because the likelihood of finding her way back decreased with every mile they traveled.

She couldn't see the shore anymore, so she feared they had gone past the edge of the island and were headed for open water. If that was the case, there was no way of knowing where the man was taking her. The boat just seemed to increase its speed until their surroundings were little more than a blur. Remembering their rescue from the dive Keilani tried to seek out the fishing boat belonging to Xavier's uncle, Tom Hawkins, but if he was anywhere close she couldn't see him. Even if she could, she wasn't sure how to get his attention, and against a SEAL, she wasn't sure he would be any help.

The horizon seemed hopelessly empty. The idea of being alone on the ocean with her abductor made her heart race until she was sick. *Think, Keilani! There has to be a way out of this.* Crazy thoughts swarmed in her head—throwing herself overboard or launching herself at him and trying to knock him off balance—but she knew she could never overpower him and leaving the boat was a sure death sentence this far out. The sharks would find her before anyone else did.

She watched his movements, wondering if he had any accomplices he would be in contact with, but he didn't seem concerned with anyone else. She had a feeling this guy was the one who wanted her dead. It seemed likely he was tired of the failed attempts of his cohorts and intended to see the job completed.

She intended to see that he failed.

Using all of her powers of reasoning, Keilani began to concoct a plan to outsmart him. What would he expect her to do? How did he plan to carry out her murder? She shuddered at the thought, but knew figuring it out was her only hope of thwarting him. If she could deduce his intentions and surprise him by doing the opposite of what he thought she would, she just might be able to get away.

But that was a very important *if.*

A little while into the boat ride, Keilani's captor turned off the GPS device he had been looking at. Was he playing some sort of mind game with her? Or had there been a sudden change of plans? He had been on his cell phone several times as well, so she suspected it was the latter.

Her stomach clenched when he pulled the mask off his head. The message couldn't be clearer. He had no intention of letting her go alive. Worse, she knew his face. He was the officer who had often come into the dolphin enclosures, the one who had tried to send Micah to the admiral while Gus was sick. Hadn't Micah said the man's marriage was struggling or something like that? She strained to remember what she knew about the man, but even his name eluded her.

She watched as the water went by, hoping for any sort of landmark—even a buoy that might help her eventually find her way back to the base should she manage to escape. The hard-eyed stare of her abductor was on her constantly, and when he realized what she was doing, he let out a cruel laugh just before his fist connected with the side of her head. She wobbled a bit in stubborn determination before everything went black.

He was hauling her off the boat when she came to, an unfamiliar bay surrounding them. Tossing her into a miserable position over his shoulder, he carted her struggling form into a dark opening beside the water, low enough that he had to duck to enter. He wasn't affected by her kicking and writhing in the least and her hopes sank further still. He seemed to possess super-human strength. Even if she could outsmart him some-how, if he ever caught her, he could simply snap her to pieces with his bare hands.

Depositing her on the rocky ground with a merciless thud, her abductor pulled out a blade that looked every bit as evil as he did. "Talk. What all do they know?"

Keilani struggled to a sitting position and shook her head. "I don't know what you mean."

He came closer and trailed the hooked end of the knife down her arm. "You won't bleed to death for a long time, but it will hurt—a lot. You can at least make your death less painful by telling me what I want to know."

Keilani's pulse was loud in her ears, her chest almost aching with the fierce pounding of her heart. "I don't know what you're asking."

He jerked in anger, slashing the blade across the surface of her forearm, leaving a trail of blood welling up in its path. It wasn't deep but it sent a searing pain coursing through her. "You know exactly what I'm ask-ing. How did you know where to find our operation? Who are you working for? Did the FBI send you?"

She let out a high-pitched laugh. "You've got it all wrong. I found it by accident. I am a civilian employed temporarily by the navy as a consultant for the marine mammal program. That's it. That's all."

"So the Feds? What do they know?" He paced away and then came back, seeming to have completely ig-nored her statement.

"How should I know?" Keilani shrugged, desperate to make him understand.

He slapped her hard. "I don't need your sarcasm. You expect me to believe you didn't report it?"

"Only to the navy. I don't know what they've done with the information." She flinched as she felt blood oozing from the corner of her mouth. He still had her wrists zip-tied together and she could do nothing except endure the sensation of it trickling down her chin.

"And what exactly have you reported to the navy? Location? Vessels you saw? People involved?" He waved the wicked-looking knife around at her again. His expression was wild.

Keilani tried to shrink away. "The only information I had was the location. I shared that. How could I know anyone involved? They were all wearing scuba gear."

He lunged at her, knife in one hand, the other at her throat. "You're lying! How else could they know I am involved?"

The expression on his face was terrifying. Keilani shook her head frantically, trying to think. How would she ever convince him she was telling the truth? What made him think the navy knew he was involved? What had she missed?

Desperation made her a little reckless. She grunted as she shoved at the knife.

"I'm telling the truth." She spat the words out forcefully.

He reacted in anger once again. The musty scent of damp rocks and brine filled her nose as he shoved her at the ground, face-first. Her cheek connected with a sharp rock and she gasped in pain.

"Who did you see on the beach?" He screamed the question in her ear and she winced.

What was he talking about? Her mind raced for answers.

"What beach?" Her air was limited, his knee in her back, but she managed the question anyway.

He smacked the back of her head, sending her forehead slamming into the rock below her. Pain exploded in her head and her vision blurred.

"I know you saw them. You had to see them leaving the dock while you were on the beach. Why else would you swim out to follow them?" His voice was strident with anger. Reasoning with him wasn't going to work. She decided to try to find out all she could instead.

"Was it Jarnigan? Was he on the beach? Did you kill him?"

His expression took on a faraway look. "I didn't kill Bax. He's my friend. He didn't deserve that. That was all on…"

He stopped and turned to stare at her. "How did you know about Bax?"

"He was a Ghost, wasn't he?" She kept her voice quiet, soothing.

"He was. Until they dismissed him. It wasn't his fault he was pulled in. Same with me. That's how they found me." He shook his head, and she decided it wasn't the time to ask about that. The answers would come.

"So you were both coerced into helping?" She made it almost a statement.

"At first. But they were so stupid, I had to take charge. They were going to get us all killed or thrown in prison. It was a matter of time. They didn't have great ideas. I figured out the dolphins."

"How many navy dolphins did you use? It must have

been hard to pull that off." She waited for the anger, but something changed in his whole demeanor.

"I should have gotten Lieutenant Kent's job. They never gave me a fair shot at it." There was a smugness to his remark that told her she had found a way to get him talking.

"Oh? Why do you say that? Didn't you get a chance to apply for the position?" It made her almost physically ill to think of this monster working with the dolphins, but she could pretend to believe it might be okay if it would buy her some time.

"The navy doesn't work like that. They have their favorites. And Micah Kent wasn't going to last as a regular SEAL. But being a favorite of our CO, they gave it to him just to save his career. I was much better with the animals." He seemed convinced he was telling the truth.

"You know, that's not really the story I heard. Maybe you can clarify what happened."

His eyes narrowed and she wondered if she had just pushed too far. "I'm sure Kent told you some dumb story about how well the dolphins liked him."

"Something like that." She tried to look confounded, like it surprised her that the reports didn't line up.

"I think our CO just told him that because he didn't have any solid reason to hire him over me. That's just how they do things sometimes." His stance alone was patronizing, chest out, chin jutted forward like he was really someone. But the way he talked to her like she was a slow-witted child made her want to give him a thorough tongue-lashing. He didn't even know the first thing about dolphins.

She managed to hide her irritation. "Oh, well, I'm

sure you were very angry with Micah, if you were better qualified for the job."

"You have no idea. And because of military protocol and all the people watching, I just had to act like I was happy for him. It was like a couple of ditzy cheerleaders trying out for the team or something."

"Squad." She absently corrected him. She was focused on the rest of what he had said.

"I knew I'd get my revenge eventually, though. It's obvious to everyone on base he's in love with you. So killing you will have multiple benefits for me. And until then, you'll be a good bargaining chip."

"But what is there really to get revenge for? I mean, you probably ended up in a better position anyway." She was trying to keep him talking about anything besides killing her. This had to work. Like he had mentioned, he was worried about appearances. She could use that to her advantage.

"Ha! Nope, I still have to work twice as hard as anyone for ungrateful citizens who sit around and wait on me to defend their freedoms."

"But you're a hero. How would it look to all those citizens to find out you killed an innocent person? You could turn in your cohorts, make a confession and still be the good guy."

"It's too late for all that. Besides, I've found out it pays better to work for someone other than Uncle Sam. In any case, they won't find your body. See that dark area of water over there just past those rocks? Dozens of sharks frequent those waters. A little blood to draw their attention and there will be nothing left of you by nightfall. Or if you'd rather, I can leave you tied in one of these caves. When the tide comes in, they fill with water. You would drown and your body would drift out to sea with the lowering tide." His laughter caused her pulse to beat hard in her neck. Keilani had the chilling thought that he was enjoying the prospects.

She needed a new plan. "How did you get involved in all this? Surely, you were a good guy when you first became a SEAL. Don't you have a wife or mother? A grandmother? A daughter? Or even a sister? Anyone at all who would want to see you continue to fight the good fight?"

He jerked her back to her feet. Watching her for a moment, he seemed to consider her words.

His face changed. "Don't you see? I'm doing this for them. The drug lord has men holding my wife and my daughter hostage until I deliver the drugs. I can't let you ruin this or they'll kill my family. I can't let that happen."

His expression turned wild again, but she tried anyway. "The navy will help you get them back without letting anything happen to them. Just turn these men in to the authorities. You'll get a lighter sentence, and—"

Something about that was the wrong thing to say. His anger returned with a vengeance and he hit her across the cheek with the back of his hand. "No more talking."

Keilani stumbled back and fell hard, unable to catch herself with her zip-tied hands. Her shoulder hit a rock and she cried out. He was on her in an instant, holding her arms against her sides and fighting her struggles as if they were nothing.

Suffocating fear like she had never known before gripped her like a vise. She couldn't breathe, only pray for mercy and a fast death. She would rather die quickly than endure whatever torture he might have in mind for her.

She heard her own scream, as if listening from afar, but then he cuffed her on the head again and blackness was all she remembered.

Micah coughed and sputtered, fighting to regain his memory. For a moment he thought he was on a training mission as he recalled hearing the voice of a fellow SEAL. However, as he remembered losing Keilani, he realized what that voice had said to him, and a sick knot formed in his stomach. The situation returned to him with a violent assault to his midsection. One of his SEAL brothers was behind this—and Dalton Taggert had taken Keilani.

Water surrounded him and he fought to keep above it. His boat was sinking beneath him and the bay around him looked deserted. If he had to swim back to shore he would lose precious time. But what choice did he have? He couldn't go after Keilani without a boat. And worse yet, he had no idea where the guy had even taken her. He grappled for other options but only for a moment. Fighting the water's pull around him was costing him precious energy. He ripped off a piece of his T-shirt and tied it tightly around his wound, then dove into the water and began to swim for shore.

The distance seemed almost insurmountable in his weakened state, but he turned off the thoughts of possible failure, numbed his mind and simply swam. Considering every problem he needed to solve right now would do nothing but overwhelm him. He needed to focus on one thing at a time, and before he could rescue Keilani and locate his dolphins, he had to get to shore and find a boat.

The tide pulled at him and the sting of salt water flooded his nose, erasing the scent of seaweed and fish with the salty brine. The cold water was a relief against his hot skin, and he could hear nothing but the white noise of the ocean around him, punctuated by the occasional cry of a gull up above. His eyes stung from the water's constant assault on his face, but it didn't matter much. There was nothing to see but empty waves.

No matter how much he tried to block it all out and focus, however, Keilani's sweet face was always there in his mind, driving his heart rate up and pushing him to go harder. She was counting on him. She needed him, and he needed her. In that instant he knew with certain clarity that he would give up all of his previous goals and expectations for his future to be with her, even if it meant sacrificing his career as a SEAL and working with the dolphins.

He loved her and would never be able to continue if he let anything happen to her. He had to find her and tell her. More than anything in that moment he wanted her to know that he loved her.

The sounds of shoreline activity gradually began to blend into the white noise. He couldn't see it, but he knew it was getting closer. He fought harder, anxious to reach the sand and move forward with his plans. He knew just where to get a fast boat, and as soon as he found sand under his feet, he was moving in the direction of the dock.

He had drifted a pretty good ways up from the base and there were a few civilians milling about this section of the beach. He hoped he would find his friend Jesse and his Baja speedboat at the dock where Jesse rented out jet skis and other water toys to tourists and occasional locals who were looking for weekend entertainment. He made his way to the shop next to the dock.

The door bounced off the wall, startling the blond, tanned young man behind the counter, but his grin grew wide when he saw Micah. "You always know how to make an entrance. You have a nice swim?"

Micah didn't take the time to respond to his friend's gibe. "Jesse, I need to borrow your boat. It's an emergency."

"Sure, man. Anything I can help with?" Jesse turned and grabbed a set of keys with a yellow foam floatation device attached to the key ring from the wall behind him. He tossed them to Micah without questioning his intent, just as Micah knew he would.

"Can you get a message to Emmett and Xavier for me? I lost my cell phone when my boat sank." He was already moving toward the dock.

Jesse raised a brow, but seemed to realize there wasn't time for Micah to explain. "Sure. What's the message?"

As Jesse followed him out, Micah told him what Xavier and the rest of the team needed to know. "Tell them I'm headed toward Pirate Bay. I have a feeling he might have taken Keilani there because he wants me to follow. Tell them to be careful who they trust. Our perp is a SEAL."

Jesse sucked in a breath. "Man, that's rough. Do you know who?" Jesse knew most of Micah's platoon-mates from hanging out with them off duty.

"I know one of them for sure, but I don't know if anyone else from the platoon is involved. I hope not, but you never know." He briefly explained what he had pieced together about the possibility of Taggert's involvement and watched Jesse's eyes widen in disbelief. He just nodded, though, and promised to have his back.

Micah jumped onto the sleek black Baja while Jesse helped him unwind the tie-out ropes from the hooks on the dock.

Jesse nodded his understanding. "Stay safe, brother."

Micah fired up the boat's engine and the entire craft shook from the powerful answering rumble. He gave Jesse a salute before easing out of the slip and giving it the full throttle. The pungent fumes disappeared in a flash as the nose took to the air and the craft shot across the water.

Step one solved, but the next question would be whether or not he was correct about where Taggert had taken Keilani. It was a good distance to Pirate Bay, a little-known area of caves and jetties that was rumored to be used for illegal activity from time to time. It seemed like the logical place for someone to take a captive. Micah only knew of the place because it was occasionally used for SEAL training since some of the caves went under water during high tide, making them nearly impossible to escape. Training there had been torture—something none of the SEALs on his team would ever forget. If he guessed right, Dalton Taggert probably had similar memories of the place.

His gut squeezed at the thought that the man intended to harm Keilani. Taggert was one of his brothers. No matter what was going on with Taggert, Micah would never want it to come to this. Whatever Taggert was involved in wasn't worth him coming to harm.

The Baja ate up the miles of water in a matter of

minutes, although it seemed much longer to Micah. The waves of the open water were daunting today, and he had to slow the boat more than he would have liked before reaching his destination. He would never reach Keilani in time if the boat capsized. When the dark shape of the rocks outlining Pirate Bay finally came into view, he wanted to speed up again, but knew better. He tamped down his impatience and kept a steady course.

The waves breaking the shore along the jagged rocks were thankfully still low and a good ways out. That was a good sign. The caves wouldn't begin to fill with water until the tide rose farther up the shore. He scanned the coastline looking for the other boat. Nothing was visible at first glance, but after another scan, Micah thought he saw a small slip of dark burgundy glinting in the sun just beyond an outcropping of rocks. He adjusted the throttle on the Baja and cruised in closer, careful not to get near enough to alert Keilani's captor of his presence. That wasn't an easy feat considering the loud rumble of the Baja's engine. He cut the motor and drifted in for a closer look.

The other boat bobbed listlessly between two out-croppings, the rocks shielding it from view at most angles and keeping the waves from battering it to pieces. He might have missed it had he not known where to look. As he drew near, Micah scanned the rocks and caves, hoping for any bit of evidence to point him in Keilani's direction. He tried to keep thoughts of being too late out of his head. If anything happened to Keilani before he could get to her, Micah hated to consider what he might do to the man in his anger.

The Baja drifted in beside the other boat and Micah threw out an anchor at the back before silently leaping out and tying off the nose to a big rock against the shore. It wasn't easy to keep quiet, considering what he wanted to do was crash the caves and demand he get Keilani back immediately. But his SEAL training won out in the end. Stealth was much more effective. It gave him the element of surprise.

He was making his way toward the first cave when all of his good intentions were nearly lost forever as Keilani's scream filled the air.

FOURTEEN

Micah felt both panic and renewed hope at the sound of Keilani's cry. It meant he wasn't too late yet, but it also meant Taggert was hurting her. He squeezed his eyes closed and prayed for her protection. Then he plunged ahead, doing his best to be quiet, but his desperate need to reach her in time was definitely complicating things. His SEAL skills were being put to the ultimate test.

Reaching the top of a boulder along the shore beside the caves, he struggled to hold his composure when he got a good look. The sight of Dalton Taggert hitting Keilani's already bruised and bleeding face caused him to lose all good sense. He wanted to do that and worse to Taggert in return for all the misery the man had caused Keilani.

But right now he had to save her.

Dalton had his SEAL-issue Ontario MK3 knife in one hand and he stood over Keilani's form, which now seemed completely inert. Panic swelled in Micah's chest. Dalton launched the weapon at the dirt beside his feet. That did nothing to comfort Micah. It was not unusual for a SEAL to kill someone without a weapon.

Being disarmed and having to use one's own strength had been a frequent occurrence in Afghanistan.

He had to use the element of surprise to his advantage, so he did his best to shut off all the flashbacks and go into attack mode.

The knife was flying through the air before Dalton even knew he was being attacked. Micah poured every bit of remaining strength he had into doing battle. Every pent-up ounce of fear and concern for Keilani, all the untested feelings for her he had kept bottled up in denial came full force into the fight. Dalton was still trying to recover from the shock of the ambush and it was apparent he hadn't expected Micah to fight with this kind of strength.

He tried to pull his Sig, but Micah easily knocked it from his hand and took him to the ground. Raining blows down on Dalton's head, Micah didn't stop until Dalton began to wail for mercy. Blood spurted from his nose and mouth, and though he had gotten a good blow or two in on Micah, he was definitely losing the fight.

"Micah, stop! You have to listen. I'm not who you think I am." Dalton shook his head and as soon as Micah's grip loosened, he managed to raise his hands up a bit in surrender.

"That's for sure. I thought we were brothers. How could you do this, man?" He tightened his grip on Dalton again, leery of making the same mistake he had made with the man in the past.

"Listen to me. I'm still one of the good guys." The look in Dalton's eyes was one of desperation.

Micah considered this for a half an instant before his gaze landed on Keilani's unmoving body again, and rage filled him. "You're lying. No matter what, you're going to pay for what you've done. You've betrayed us all."

Micah wanted to keep pummeling the man, but it was doing no good. He couldn't even feel satisfaction for avenging Keilani's injuries knowing his brother in arms had turned on them all.

Dalton lay completely still, the blows having rendered him unconscious, but even as Micah stood, he felt the aftershocks as if he was still fighting. All for money, this man had become a traitor of the worst sort. And though Micah had always been sickened by the very idea of it, having someone he trusted so completely turn on him and everyone he held dear in his life was even worse than he had imagined.

He barely got Dalton tied up securely before his stomach rebelled on him. When he had thrown up the contents of his stomach, he hurried to Keilani's side. She began to stir just a little, but she stayed on her side, balled up like a terrified child.

The bruises and open cuts on her face and arms made him want to finish Dalton off, but he knew he couldn't do it. He would rather see the drug operation stopped and have Dalton pay for his deeds. The man would have to see the stares of all of his betrayed brothers on him while he stood trial for his crimes. He was the ultimate disgrace.

Focusing on Keilani, Micah gently spoke to her, afraid to try to move her until he knew the extent of her injuries. She only moved her head and mumbled at first, but gradually she began to blink, and finally opened her eyes.

"Micah? Am I dreaming?" She tried to push herself up, but immediately cried out in pain.

"Take it easy now. Is it all right if I pick you up? We need to get you to a hospital." He stroked her hair back away from her face and gently smoothed the strands. He examined her carefully, not willing to rely only on what she told him in the state she was in. He wouldn't move her until he knew it was safe. But questioning her would keep her talking.

She moaned. "I think so. It's so hard to tell. I hurt everywhere."

He began to look her over. Bruises seemed to be popping up everywhere, just as she said, and when he used the knife to carefully cut the zip ties from her wrists, she cried out. There were deep, angry red indentations where they had been so tightly locked around her wrists. He rubbed at them gently, trying to restore healthy blood flow, though he knew the tingling was painful in her hands. She winced and he apologized.

"I know. It hurts, but it will feel better soon." He noticed the gash on her arm, then, too, and sucked in a breath. "That might need stitches."

Keilani gave him a weak smile. "How did you find me?"

Micah slid his arms under her and gathered her to him with a careful tenderness he hadn't known he possessed. The last thing he would want to do was hurt her more. "Just an educated guess."

She leaned into him, relaxing against his body. "I thought for sure you weren't going to escape. He left you on a sinking boat and there was nothing I could do. I was so afraid you would drown."

The tears welled in her eyes and he was almost undone by the knowledge that, despite all the pain she was in herself, the thing that brought her to tears was her concern for him. He would do anything to make her smile again.

"Hey, where's your faith in me? I'm a SEAL, remember?" He looked down at her, nestled in his arms, and gave her a crooked grin.

It had the desired effect, though her smile was still full of pain. "How could I forget?"

"Let's get you out of here."

A sudden stunning blow caught Micah at the base of his skull before he could take a step. He crumpled, almost falling on top of Keilani. He managed to twist and land on his side instead.

"I guess I should have just put a bullet in you both when I had the chance. Now look what you've done." Blood ran down both sides of Dalton's face. The victorious ring was still present in his voice as he gestured to the tide coming in. The Sig and Dalton's vicious knife were lost somewhere in the incoming waves.

"I guess I'll just have to leave you to the tide. Good thing I was prepared for this. Oh, who am I kidding? I was hoping for this." He grabbed Keilani around the throat and turned her to face Micah, who was still reeling from the debilitating blow. The pressure he was putting on her throat was turning her face red, and Micah had no doubt the man could easily kill her.

He stood slowly and put his hands in the air. He was at a disadvantage again—the worst kind, really, since the two men had been trained in exactly the same manner. There wouldn't be a single trick Micah knew that Dalton hadn't been taught, as well. And there was no doubt in either of their minds who was the strongest of the two. The only advantage Micah had over him was intelligence. The ability to think on his feet would have to save them.

Keilani whimpered and Micah could see the hope fading from her eyes. He knew what she had to be thinking. *When will this be over? Will I have to die before it ends?* He wanted desperately to end it for her. It was like this guy had the multiple lives of a feline. He wouldn't stay down, no matter what.

"Okay, Kent, get over there against the wall of the cave. Right there by the hooks. Make one wrong move and I'll snap her neck. The tide is coming in, and we both know how fast this cave floods. Once I have you both secured, I'll leave you to drown in misery together. You should have just enough time to confess your undying love before you go under for good."

The biting sarcasm in his voice left little doubt as to his feelings on the matter. He shoved Keilani up against the wall beside Micah and tied them together, separately, and then to a metal hook that had been drilled into the solid rock wall of the cave.

"You see, Kent. In training they made it easy for us to get out, although if I remember correctly, you had more trouble than most. You always were our weakest link. But this time I'm going to make it impossible for you to escape." His deep laugh resounded throughout the cave, like the ominous sound effects in a horror movie.

Micah shook off the disparaging remarks. He wasn't the same guy he'd been way back then. But let Dalton believe it. Maybe it would make him careless enough to give them a means of escape. It stung for Keilani to hear of his failures, but he had worse problems at the moment.

He wanted to reassure Keilani somehow, but he didn't want to give Dalton any advantages. He did his best to silently communicate with her through his eyes. They would be okay. He would find a way to get them out of this.

Micah had to admit it was looking bleak, though. The tide was already beginning to seep into the cave, the ominous sounds of dribbling water echoing through the dank cavern. Dalton stood back and swiped his hands together like he was dusting them off, looking entirely too pleased with himself.

"Let's see you get out of that. I don't think you'll have time. And if you do, you'll have to choose to let her die to come after me, or stay here and die trying to free her before it's too late. I'm pretty sure I know what you'll do."

"You can kill us, but we aren't the only ones who know. You won't be safe for long." Keilani was beginning to babble nervously. Micah shook his head at her. It wouldn't do any good. She was just bluffing, anyway, since she didn't even realize he had asked Jesse to send Xavier a message.

"You may not be the only ones who know, but I'll be long gone before the rest of them figure out what happened." He smirked. "I've got a nice little island set up waiting for me where I can retire from all this."

The water was beginning to flow into the cave a little higher with every pulsing wave. Micah was already trying to figure out what might work to get them free. He could work the zip ties off if they were only around his wrist, but the way Dalton had entangled Micah's and Keilani's zip ties together, he'd have to talk her through it. To do that, he needed Dalton to leave. He seemed in no hurry, however, as he watched the froth of water roll into the cave.

"You know, I was actually a little frightened the day

we had to do this training exercise. I used to suffer from a bit of claustrophobia. Ever have that problem?" Taggert leaned in toward Keilani, watching her closely. Had he been spying on them when she had told Micah about her fear?

He was enjoying her panic. It made Micah even more furious. But he was proud of her, when she merely lifted her chin and stared at him, denying him the pleasure of seeing her fear.

It must have annoyed Dalton when she didn't give him the desired response. He frowned. "Whatever. Have fun with this little puzzle. I'm out."

A sigh of relief escaped Micah when he disappeared from the low-ceilinged cave. "Finally. We have to work together and work fast."

Keilani squeaked out a reply. "Just tell me what to do."

Micah began to explain his plan as he worked at their wrists, instructing her carefully on how to turn her hands and what to do.

"Move your right wrist as close as you can get it to mine but still off the wall. You'll have to keep your left wrist close but out of the way. Twist them clockwise." He kept talking to her until she cried out in surprise.

"It hurts. I don't know if I can. He has them so tight." Her chest was heaving, though he was sure it was from the adrenaline more than anything. The water was above their ankles and rising very quickly.

"You can do this, Keilani. I know it's going to hurt, but if you can stand it for a little bit, it will be worth it when we are free." Micah spoke gently. "If you can hold it until I can work my wrists free, I will find a way to get yours off. But we have to get one of us free first."

Micah could feel the tension coming from Keilani

as she held her hands where he asked her to. He knew she was struggling. He hated knowing this was hurting her, but there was no other way.

He was beginning to feel the zip ties slide up his hands, so he kept working diligently, but a sudden rush of water crashed into the cave, throwing off his balance. He lost all progress. Biting back a sigh of frustration, he began again. The water was almost past his knees now and he knew it would start weighing them down and messing with their balance more the higher it got. This would only grow more difficult if he didn't hurry.

"Please, Micah. Can we try something else?" Keilani's voice was full of anguish. He could just imagine how much the biting of the zip ties was hurting.

"Can you think of anything else to try?" He let her relax her hands for a moment, since he was going to have to start again anyway.

"Maybe I can slip my hands out instead? You could tell me how to do it. I can try again if you'll explain how to do it correctly."

"We can try. But I have to warn you, it's pretty painful no matter how you do it and your hands and wrists won't be the same for a while. The best option would be to break them." He didn't want to discourage her, but it was difficult for some of the strongest men he knew to break industrial zip ties like these, and he had no idea if someone as dainty as Keilani could manage it.

"Tell me what to do." She sounded determined, her courage renewed at the relief from the earlier pain.

"First you have to put pressure on the zip ties. They will stretch eventually if you put pressure on them for long enough. Then, if there is any way you can get them tighter, do it. Keep doing that as many times as you can and it will weaken the plastic."

"Tighter? That makes no sense." Keilani sounded confused.

"Actually, it does. It makes the locking mechanism on the zip ties easier to break," Micah explained. "And I think breaking them might be our only option."

"I can't possibly break these. I'm not as strong as you." Keilani let up on the pressure.

"You don't have to be strong. It just takes a lot of force. The trick is finding a way to apply force in the situation we are in." Since their hands were tied together and to the wall, they couldn't use momentum against their bodies to break them. He would have to come up with another way.

"Are you sure?" He could tell she was getting nervous about the rapidly rising water.

"Yes. We might be able to work together and use our shared bodyweight to break them. If we can get the timing down, maybe we can both get free at once." He twisted as far as he could to examine the exact workings of their adversary's attempts to keep them captive. He knew there was a flaw in his plan somewhere.

Calming Keilani was going to become a necessity, however, if the water kept rising. She was breathing at a rapid pace, her shallow breaths indicating she needed reassurance. "Do you think the water will fill up the cave completely?"

Was now the best time to tell her it would? That was probably something that should wait. But how could he answer honestly? "If we work quickly we should be gone long before it becomes a concern."

Avoidance. He would explain later. For now they had to get out of here.

She began to pull at the zip ties again. "How much stretching do you think it will take to break these?"

"I have an idea." Micah had noticed as she pulled at the zip ties that the bolt in the rock wall had wobbled a tiny bit, indicating it wasn't in the rock as securely as it had once been. "I think we might be able to pull away from the wall. Then it will be easier to get out of the zip ties."

He explained to her what he was seeing, a single ring bolted into the rock that had another zip tie fastening it to the ones on their wrists. If it was loose, or stripped out, as he suspected, they could probably use their combined weight to generate enough force to pull it from the rock. Since Dalton hadn't secured their feet, it should be easy enough to use their legs as leverage if they could maneuver into a good position to do so.

"So we just want to push on the wall until the bolt gives way?" Keilani looked unconvinced.

"It may not give right away, but with continued effort, I think we might be able to dislodge it. But we have to hurry."

She eyed the swirling water once more, rising almost to her waist, and nodded. "Let's give it a try."

He let her get one foot in position before twisting awkwardly into a leveraged spot of his own. "On the count of three, give it all you've got."

He counted down and they both tugged for all they were worth. The loop gave a little, but didn't fall free of the wall. "Again on three."

The same results occurred the next four tries. He could sense Keilani was getting frustrated and wanted to give up. He suspected the bolt was at least halfway out of the wall now, though, and wasn't quitting that easily.

"Can you try just a few more times?"

She winced, but gave a succinct nod. "Yes. Say when."

They tried two more times with little result. "This isn't working." Keilani looked near to tears. Her eyes focused on the water creeping higher up her body with every breath she took.

"Just stay with me. We are getting there. Just another try or two and if it doesn't come loose, we'll try something else." Micah spoke low and calm, close to her ear. Should he be taking this time to confess his feelings? Would this be the last of their moments spent together?

No, he wouldn't waste time and energy thinking like that. He gave her a reassuring nod and counted down again. She let out a scream of frustration when they got the same result. Maybe he could motivate her a little. It wasn't ideal, but he really needed her to keep trying.

"Keilani, look at me for a second."

She did as he asked, and when her beautiful dark eyes intersected with his, he almost couldn't get the words out. "I love you. I know I have told you I never wanted to marry, but you've changed things for me. You've changed everything. We have to get out of this mess so we can spend the rest of our lives together."

To his surprise, she grew angry. "That's a dirty trick to play, Micah Kent. You know I have feelings for you, and you want to go and use them against me in a situation like this? I'm doing my best. You don't have to lie to me to get us free."

He gaped at her for a moment. "What? I'm not lying to you. I wanted to tell you as soon as we got free, but I couldn't wait any longer."

"Are—are you sure? Why?" Tears welled in her eyes.

"Yeah, I'm sure. There's nothing I want more in my life than you. I'll give up being a SEAL if that's what it takes. My life would be empty without you in it." He looked into her eyes, willing her to see the sincerity there.

"But what about the dolphins?" She gasped. Was she only just remembering they hadn't been able to rescue them yet? Maybe that would motivate her.

"If we don't get out of here, there won't be any concern there. But there will always be someone willing to take good care of them." Micah was shaking his head.

"You'd give up the dolphins for me?" She looked shell-shocked.

"Absolutely." He didn't even flinch.

She gave him a huge grin. "It's a good thing I'd never ask you to, then."

He leaned close, kissing her very gently. "On the count of three?"

With her renewed energy, their efforts doubled. This time the bolt wrenched free and Micah had to duck to keep from being smacked in the face with it. Keilani cheered in response.

"Okay, now all we need to do is break these ties and we are out of here." Micah looked around at the water pulling at them. It was up to his abdomen and seemed to be rising more quickly with every second.

He explained to Keilani what to do. He wanted her to break her ties first so that he wouldn't hurt her wrists breaking the zip ties from his own. He would never forgive himself if he broke her wrist or something.

"You're going to have to pull your knee above the water to use as leverage against the zip ties. You'll bring our hands down hard against your leg just above your knee and pull out at the same time. Hopefully, they will snap." Micah gestured the best he could with their hands bound together.

"Okay. Ready?" Keilani looked at him and then back at their hands when he nodded.

She raised her knee as high as she could while lifting her hands. He could feel her shaking now. He tried to silently will some calm into her. This had to work.

She brought their hands down with a sharp cry, but the ties didn't break. Micah's chest constricted. What if this didn't work with their hands tied together?

He pushed the doubts aside. "Try again. You can do this."

Strain was evident on her face. The water was rising so rapidly that she could barely get her knee high enough above it now. When she brought her hands down this time, though, a snap issued from the ties and she was free. His ties instantly released from hers as well, and he wasted no time breaking them from his wrists.

"Let's get out of here." He pointed to the rapidly closing mouth of the cave and they both began swimming. There was now only about a foot and a half of daylight above the water at the low opening and it was still a few yards away. The cave was low and long and their captor had been sure to put them as far from the entrance as possible. The current rushing into the crevices made it even more difficult to swim in the small space. Keeping her just in front of him, Micah encouraged Keilani the whole way out.

"The opening is closing fast. You'll likely have to swim below the surface to get under. Wait until you get close, though, so you don't miss the mouth." Micah had to raise his voice to be heard over the echoing water noise in the cave.

Keilani gave him a look that conveyed her terror, but she kept moving. This was going to be close.

FIFTEEN

Keilani couldn't breathe, but it was mostly because she was terrified. All the years of being locked up in small spaces as punishment had come back to haunt her with a fury. When the zip ties hadn't broken the first time, sheer panic had threatened to overwhelm her. If not for Micah's patient instructions, she might have just given up and waited to drown. Somehow, his faith in her inspired her to keep trying.

The water was high, pushing and pulling at her like an adversary, trying to keep her a captive to the suffocating cave. It smelled of briny water, musty rocks and fish, and she could taste the salt as it splashed her in the face here and there. It was cold, but not numbing, just enough to make her shiver in the dank, pressing water. It would have been so easy to give in to her terror and just curl into a ball to let the water overtake her.

But Micah had said he loved her. That alone was enough reason to keep fighting. Squeezing her eyes closed for a moment, she tried to picture what life might be like with him. She would never ask him to give up being a SEAL, as he had suggested. Could they work together with the dolphins long-term? Her position was supposed to be temporary. There was no way she could stay on as a consultant for the navy forever. Would she be able to find another job near the naval base? She might not be able to work with marine mammals, but surely she could find a veterinary position of some sort. And wouldn't having Micah's arms to come home to be worth it?

She thought of his kiss and how tender and magical it had been, and it gave her new strength. She would fight to her last breath for that feeling alone. She could overcome this crippling fear if it meant forever with Micah.

The opening of the cave was close now and discouraging in its smallness. The idea of passing through it seemed even more threatening now that she was close. The reflection of the close roof mocked her as she prepared to swim through, as if it warned her that she couldn't do it. Could she make it to the other side before the panic overtook her? What if she lost it and sucked in a mouthful of water? She would surely drown.

"Keilani, you can do it. I have seen you do some amazing things, and this is just one more to add to your list. We're running out of time." His voice was gentle, soft, even, in the loud cavern. It was barely audible enough for her to hear it, yet it resonated somewhere deep in her soul.

She backed toward him. "You go first."

He shook his head. "I can't do that. I need to see you safely out before I go." He made some sort of sign she decided must be the SEAL version of Scouts' honor.

She took a deep breath. "You're sure?"

He nodded and repeated his earlier words. "You can do this."

Breathing a quick prayer, Keilani squeezed her eyelids tightly and dove. Time was slowed down in her mind for the moment and it seemed like she was never going to reach the other side. Panic settled on her just as she broke the surface. She gulped in air, gasping in relief. For a moment she could only inhale the open air, but then she realized Micah wasn't surfacing. Where was he?

She waited, thinking maybe he just hadn't had time to clear the mouth of the cave yet, but as the seconds ticked by, she felt a knot of dread beginning to settle in her stomach. He should be surfacing by now. The cave was almost completely submerged, and she had no idea where he could be. She only had to debate for a moment before she dove back below the surface to search for him.

She didn't see him at first, but then she realized he was struggling with something under the water. Swimming closer, she saw he was stuck on a small outcropping of rock. He twisted this way and that, but to no avail. She swam closer, the salt water stinging her eyes, and tried to find the source of the problem. His pants had snagged on the rock and a large tear had appeared in a cargo pocket, but it had somehow wound itself around a sharp point on the rock. She couldn't fathom how it had happened, but she knew he was going to need help.

She grasped at the fabric, pulling in one direction and then another, with little success. The rock was protruding through the hole and didn't want to let go. She was running out of air fast and it was a long way to the surface. Micah had to be close to drowning. Desperate, she gave a fierce tug, then another, until the fabric ripped free of the rock. They both shot to the surface at warp speed, heaving in great breaths of air.

"That was close." Micah lay on his back and just floated for a moment while he inhaled breath after breath. "I owe you my life."

Keilani shook her head, breathing hard, as well. "I consider it a small repayment for all the times you've saved mine."

He raised up. "Let's get out of here. We still have some dolphins to find."

Keilani's forehead creased. "Yes. Are you sure you're okay?"

Micah tried to grin. "Yeah. I've been through worse."

She rolled her eyes. "Lead the way, then."

Thankfully, the Baja speedboat Micah must have arrived on was still there. Either Dalton didn't expect them to escape, or he was in too big of a hurry to reach his island to worry about it. Micah briefly wondered aloud about a bomb, but decided Dalton probably hadn't been prepared for that. Explosives would have been more obvious if he had the means to make them in this case.

Keilani was thankful for his help getting into the boat. She was already feeling the effects of the abuse she had taken at the hands of her captor, and she tried not to wince as he sped out of the cove over jostling waves.

She imagined her physical pain was just a reflection of the emotional pain he was likely feeling right now over his dolphins. But she was worried about them, too. Would they be safe until Keilani and Micah could find them? They had never been on their own, or at least not recently enough to remember it. Her education told her that the dolphins' instincts would likely see them through, but would it be soon enough to keep them out of harm's way?

Micah's story about the dolphins was touching, and Keilani suspected he had only scratched the surface of what those cetaceans meant to him. She would do everything she possibly could to help see them all safely returned to the naval base.

When she realized he was heading back toward the base instead of out to sea, she questioned him, having to shout to be heard over the roaring boat motor. "Where are you going? We need to find the dolphins."

He shook his head. "No one is safe until we catch Dalton. I'm taking him down."

She knew her shock must have shown on her face. "But those dolphins—they're your babies."

"I can't take another chance on him getting away. I have to get him this time." Micah's face was a hard mask.

She didn't argue further. She only hoped they weren't too late. Her captor could be on his way to that remote island he told them about by now. How would Micah react if he was gone?

She didn't have to find out. They reached the dock and found the maroon boat they were looking for almost as soon as they arrived. Micah didn't even take time to tie off the boat properly, but threw a nearby dock worker the rope and launched himself off the boat. He landed on top of Dalton before the man knew what hit him. He was still unconscious, Micah holding him tightly by the throat, when a whole fleet of men—SEALs, from the looks of them—ran out onto the dock.

Keilani nearly fainted with relief to see Xavier among them. After a few words with Micah, the men had Dalton Taggert tied securely and were hauling him away. Xavier was the last to leave, speaking to Micah for a moment before leaving with the rest of the men.

Micah stood where they had left him, heaving and staring at her. She almost expected him to collapse.

She didn't think, only ran into his arms. The stunned kid on the dock still stood staring after them both, holding on to the rope of the bobbing Baja. Keilani didn't even care as she kissed Micah with every ounce of energy she had left. He kissed her back with a wild tenderness that she relished.

"You're safe." He whispered the words against her lips. "Xavier said they have all of his accomplices in custody. They were about to ambush him and come after us, but they were trying to confirm Dalton was the one. I didn't tell them they would have been too late to save us."

She only sighed and fell into him, not able to find the words to express her relief. There was only one thing she could think of to say, only one emotion dominating her thoughts.

"I love you, Lieutenant Micah Kent."

He smiled broadly and kissed her again. "I love you, Dr. Keilani Lucas."

"Let's go find your dolphins."

They didn't waste any time. As soon as they could report to the admiral about everything that had happened and all Dalton had said to Keilani, they were off again to look for the dolphins. A crew from investigations was currently looking for Dalton's wife and daughter, though he didn't have much hope that they would be found alive. It softened the gut punch just a little to know that Dalton had begun this betrayal with the intent of protecting those he held dear. But he should have known better. He should have trusted his brothers to help him get his family back. He knew there were probably reasons Dalton felt the SEAL team couldn't have overcome the drug lord he had gotten mixed up with, but Micah was sure they could have.

Watching Keilani in the weak afternoon light, he

knew he would do whatever it took to keep her safe, but he also understood his SEAL brothers would do the same. Every man on the team would do that much for any loved one of any other member. Where had they lost Dalton's trust? It was a troubling question.

The afternoon had seemed eternal. The sun was setting over the bay and it was one of the most beautiful sights Micah had ever seen. Why had he never taken the time to appreciate the beauty around him more? He looked at Keilani and knew she was the reason he was noticing now. She had done something remarkable to him. It was almost like he had become a new person in the past few days.

He had noticed her praying on more than one occasion. It made him wonder what had happened to his own faith. He decided right then to make a renewed effort to prioritize his Lord. Keilani smiled at him as if she knew what he was thinking.

"I've been praying for your dolphins." She looked a little embarrassed at the admission. "If I am right, I think I see them now."

She pointed off in the distance, and sure enough, he could see an occasional splash following a graceful arc over the water. It might not be them, but his heart raced at the thought that it could be.

After Micah had informed the admiral of all that they knew, the navy insisted on sending along a much bigger boat for transport, hoping to pull in as many dolphins at a time as possible.

The boat actually hadn't been designed as such, but thanks to some brilliant navy engineers, it was converted into one for dolphin transport in less than an hour. It followed at a sedate pace, so Micah wasn't getting there as fast as he would have liked. At the sight of the dolphins, however, he increased the throttle and aimed right for them, ignoring the lagging transport boat behind them.

He slowed as they got close, then cut the motor. He gave a shrill whistle, and within seconds several sleek dolphins rocketed toward them like torpedoes. A nose popped up next to the starboard side of the boat and Micah couldn't stop a smile of relief.

"Nikita! How's my girl? You're a long way from home, aren't you?" He ran a hand down the side of her head, and she clicked and squeaked in response. A few more silvery noses broke the surface and Micah greeted the dolphins by name.

Keilani watched them for a moment, smiling as well, and then came over to the side. "My, my! You kids have been out on quite the adventure today, haven't you?"

"It's time to go home." Micah gave them a stern look, and a couple of them lowered their noses to play shy as if they understood.

Sweet, tender emotion swelled within him and when he looked at Keilani, she was watching his face. He was more than just relieved that she was okay. It meant everything to him.

She spoke in a low voice as the transport boat drew close. "Careful. You're going to lose your reputation as a tough-as-nails navy SEAL."

Her eyes were smiling and he knew she was teasing him. "I don't even care right now." He was smiling right back. "I'm getting my babies back."

By the time the dolphins had all been returned to base, Keilani was near collapse. She had never been so mentally and physically exhausted in her whole life. She did, however, utter a prayer of thanks that the dolphins had all been recovered and seemed to be perfectly healthy. It was absolutely amazing that they hadn't lost a single one.

"Dr. Lucas, the admiral requests to meet with you at oh-seven-hundred tomorrow morning." The young woman didn't look her in the eye, but Keilani agreed and thanked her before the uniformed private scuttled off.

"I guess your mission is complete." Micah stood close behind her, and she felt a squeeze of bittersweet relief at his presence. She was happy to be so close to him, but feared what might happen now. Would this be the last time she saw him? "Maybe you've completed your purpose here? I was hoping there might be a reason for you to stay on."

"Do you think I'm going to be let go, then? That I am no longer needed without a problem to solve?" Keilani was more than a little disappointed, almost panicked.

"I don't know. I guess we will just have to see what he has to say. But he requested to talk to you, and he admitted you have completed your original purpose here."

Keilani nodded. "So I'm going to be fired."

"Not fired. Dismissed." He was scowling so hard it made *her* jaw hurt.

"Back to Hawaii for me, then, I suppose." Her chest squeezed. She had no reason to stay unless Micah gave her one. He seemed to be a different person now that they were back on base.

"There is one other option." He stared at her intently.

"Oh? And what might that be?" She knew she shouldn't get her hopes up. He had said he loved her, but it had been an emotional moment. A relationship took time…

"Stay. I know you probably don't want to wait around

on a SEAL to complete active duty, but I would love it if you would. I have to finish out my enlistment, but after that I can apply for early retirement and find a civilian job. It would be a couple of years. But if you'd be willing to wait—well, I want to marry you."

She tried to hold back her smile. "And what if I don't want to wait around on you to be finished?"

"I guess I understand that. It's one of the reasons why I always said I wouldn't marry. I had just hoped…"

"You'd just hoped what, Lieutenant Kent? That I'd be content to sit around and wait to hear if you were coming home from your latest mission in one piece? That I would hang around and hope that one day your career might be over and you might marry me? What if I just don't like to wait?"

He looked shocked. "I know we were close to dying there for a while, Keilani, but you said some things and I thought you meant them."

"You mean, like how I love you?"

He nodded. "Yeah. Like that."

"I did mean them."

"Then what…?"

She threw her arms around him. "I just don't want to wait a couple of years. And you don't have to give up being a SEAL for me, either, Micah Kent. Do what you love. Just love me, too. That's all I ask. I'm not afraid of being a SEAL wife."

His expression eased. "You're sure?"

"I'm absolutely sure."

He kissed her until her world was spinning. "I'm absolutely sure, too."

EPILOGUE

The wedding was on a Saturday morning on the Coronado Naval Base with every single navy dolphin in attendance. Keilani walked the brightly lit walkway above the dolphin training pool that had recently been built outside along the beach.

At Keilani's suggestion, the navy had included more sunshine in the dolphins' lives by providing them turnout time in a beachside enclosure complete with toys for the dolphins to interact with, much as they might have in the ocean itself. It was the most beautiful thing they had done since she had accepted the permanent position the admiral had offered her as a civilian consultant and public relations director for the marine mammal program. He hadn't wanted to dismiss her after all, but upgrade her position status from temporary to permanent. Micah was the only person happier about it than Keilani.

Xavier and Emmett stood up with Micah, and the rest of the SEAL team was crowded around close. The team had been so appalled at what Dalton Taggert had done that it had taken no time at all to have him sentenced to life in prison, along with being stripped of all rank and position as a SEAL. There was very nearly a mutiny before it could be properly handled. The report from his lawyer was that he had been drugged and coerced into working for the drug lord when he had been caught alone on the beach one night in the wee hours. No matter what his excuse, he would never be forgiven by the team.

Keilani had flown her grandparents in for the wedding and her best friend, Jacquie, from the islands, as well. Jacquie stood as maid of honor, and if Keilani wasn't mistaken, she had captured the attention of more than one man on the SEAL team, Emmett included.

She had called her mother, too, thinking that news of her engagement might bring her around at last, but her mother had told her she simply couldn't fly to California for the wedding. Keilani had been horribly disappointed, but decided she had done all she could do.

She was more than a little surprised when she was walking back down the aisle arm in arm with her new husband and spotted her mother in the back. She stopped Micah in the middle of the aisle and headed toward her.

"Mother? I thought you weren't coming? I would have had you escorted to the front and seated in a place of honor." Keilani pulled her into a hug.

Her mother returned her embrace, albeit a little stiffly. "I didn't deserve that. It was a last-minute decision anyway. I couldn't miss my only daughter's wedding."

"I'm so glad you didn't. Mother, this is Lieutenant Micah Kent." She beamed at her new husband while she introduced them. She wasn't sure when the uniform had stopped bothering her, but now she was proud to have her husband wear it. "Micah, this is my mother, Saraiah Johnston."

The two shook hands, and then Micah pulled her small frame into an embrace. "I'm so glad you decided to come."

Her mother answered with a tiny smile. "Me, too."

It wasn't until after the reception that Saraiah finally told them the truth. "I'll be here when you get back from your honeymoon. I decided when George wouldn't let me come to the wedding that I wasn't going back. I'm filing for divorce and starting over. All of the things you've been trying to tell me finally sank in."

Keilani's heart swelled at her mother's words. "I am so proud of you. I will be thrilled to have you here with us. I can't wait for you to be a part of my life again."

Tears fell from her mother's eyes. "I missed you so much. All out of fear. Now I can never get those years with you back."

Keilani nodded. "We will do everything we can to make up for it."

They hugged for several seconds, until Keilani finally turned back to Micah. "We'd better get going."

Micah led her away to the waiting car, but as they moved toward the future together, Keilani's heart swelled with wonder. How could it be that in a few short hours she had received the answer to all of her most heartfelt prayers? It was like every dream she had ever wished for had come to pass and now she was so filled with bliss she couldn't describe it.

Micah leaned in and kissed her as he settled beside her in the car. "This is just the beginning."

"Then I can't imagine how my heart will hold the rest of the story without bursting. I'm so happy right now." She held his hand and stared into his eyes, seeing her own love reflected back there.

"I love you, Keilani. I intend to see you this happy for the rest of your life."

She whispered, "I love you, too," against his lips just before he kissed her once more.

It was going to be a beautiful life.

* * * * *

If you enjoyed this book, pick up these other exciting stories from Love Inspired Suspense.

Tracking a Kidnapper
by Valerie Hansen

Hidden Witness
by Shirlee McCoy

Alaskan Showdown
by Sarah Varland

Fatal Ranch Reunion
by Jaycee Bullard

Accidental Target
by Theresa Hall

Find more great reads at www.LoveInspired.com

Dear Reader,

Thank you for joining in Micah and Keilani's story. Micah didn't believe he was capable of being everything he wanted—a SEAL as well as a family man. Keilani's gentleness helped him see he was much more than he believed.

I love dolphins. Their intelligence, speed and playfulness make them intriguing. I'm thankful that there are loving people acting as stewards for them. Through research, I found that military dolphins receive some of the best care of any mammals around. They are brave heroes. There is debate over the use of dolphins for national defense. I have found no evidence they are put in harm's way. They enjoy interacting with humans and form quite a bond with their handlers.

I would love to hear from readers. Reach me by email at ssmith.kgc3@gmail.com or by mail at PO Box 1824, Muldrow, OK 74948.

Blessings and love,
Sommer Smith

Get 4 FREE REWARDS!

We'll send you 2 FREE Books plus 2 FREE Mystery Gifts.

Love Inspired Suspense books showcase how courage and optimism unite in stories of faith and love in the face of danger.

FREE
Value Over
$20